LOVE ME NO MORE

Faced by the prospect of bringing up her baby on her own, Berris Martindale agreed to a proposition put to her by her ex-boss, Dr. Elliott Manley. He will marry her and bring up the child as his own, if she will make a home for his sister, Dympna, who is being discharged from a psychiatric hospital. Berris decides to accept, but it is only after she meets Dympna that she realises she has taken on frightening responsibilities.

Books by Mary Jane Warmington
in the Linford Romance Library:

NURSE VICTORIA
WILD POPPY
THE STRANGERS AT BRIERY HALL
MISTRESS OF ELVAN HALL
THE FALLS OF LINGARRY
PAINTERWOOD

MARY JANE WARMINGTON

LOVE ME NO MORE

Complete and Unabridged

LINFORD
Leicester

First published in Great Britain

First Linford Edition
published 2001

British Library CIP Data

Warmington, Mary Jane
Love me no more.—Large print ed.—
Linford romance library
1. Love stories
2. Large type books
I. Title
823.9′14 [F]

ISBN 0–7089–9711–2

Published by
F. A. Thorpe (Publishing)
Anstey, Leicestershire

Set by Words & Graphics Ltd.
Anstey, Leicestershire
Printed and bound in Great Britain by
T. J. International Ltd., Padstow, Cornwall

This book is printed on acid-free paper

1

I was cold.

I sat on an outcrop and contemplated the fells, always majestic and colourful whatever the weather. Today they were as cold and grey as Dr. Manley's eyes when I handed in my resignation.

I had expected very little protest beyond minor irritation and a request to pass on my work to Susan Crawley, but in this I was wrong. Dr. Manley flicked a switch on the intercom and asked for all telephone calls to be held for precisely five minutes.

'Sit down, Miss Martindale.'

I sat down.

'You want more money?'

'No, Dr. Manley. I . . . I just want to leave . . . '

'To be married?'

I swallowed, feeling the warm colour touching my cheeks.

'No, Dr. Manley. Please . . . I just want to give in my notice. I'm going home to Cumbria . . .'

He stared at me, his eyes owl-like behind horn-rimmed spectacles, his black hair neatly brushed, his face long and lean with high cheek bones. Only once had I seen him without the spectacles, when we had been driving through the streets of Honolulu and the rays of the sun had forced him to remove them for dark shades.

'Let me see . . . I understood you are now without family . . . that your aunt had died. I seem to remember that when you were asked to come with us to Malamba Island . . .'

'Yes, sir. I am alone.'

I hoped desperately for something which would turn off the inquisition. I hadn't been expecting it. Elliott Manley showed so little interest in anything or anybody not immediately connected with the job on hand that I often wondered if he had any sort of life beyond Metallurgy.

On this, his own subject, he was expert and part of his contribution to Technology was applying his considerable knowledge to finding out the causes of air crashes. For a number of years he had been attached to a London University, but now he was doing experimental work on new metals with a large industrial company. They also employed me.

Three months ago a huge airliner on a non-stop flight between Chicago, Illinois and Honolulu had crashed on Malamba Island, killing over one hundred and fifty people, passengers and crew members. Dr. Manley had been called in by an insurance company, together with other technologists to examine the wreckage, and besides his personal secretary, Stella Britton, I had been detailed to join the secretarial staff.

I was a fast and accurate typist, with reams of reports to get through while Stella dealt with letters and appointments.

Dr. Manley wished to consult some of the officials, so we flew to Chicago, then boarded another '747' jet en route for Honolulu. The plane was built on three levels, the upper deck having a delightful lounge and in case we got bored with such scenery as the Rocky Mountains, Grand Canyon or the Californian Desert, we could watch a two-hour film, or listen to music.

The journey took ten hours and Dr. Manley spent eight of the ten dictating letters to Stella and reports to me. He did not believe in sacrificing his present work for specialised jobs. He changed his dark business clothes for a lighter suit when we arrived at Honolulu where he had to spend a day or two before going by boat to Malamba, but the more casual clothing did little towards relaxing Dr. Manley. He still looked stiffly correct, his hair perfectly groomed and his expression as dedicated as ever. I was afraid of him. I felt intimidated and worried that my work would not come up to standard. The other typists in the office had family commitments, but I had recently moved to London after Aunt Grace died, and I was left alone in Highfield, a cottage on the Uldale Road from Lake Bassenthwaite. I had let the cottage to summer visitors, arranging with Mrs. Shorrocks, a friend of Aunt Grace's, to supervise the letting, and had come south to London to try to build a life for myself.

Stella had recommended me to Dr. Manley and he sent for me one afternoon.

'You've no family, Miss Martindale?'

'No, sir. I lived with my aunt, but she died a few months ago.'

He didn't make the conventional comment that he was sorry, but cleared his throat.

'No one likely to be embarrassed or deprived if you accompany us on the Malamba investigation?'

My heart jerked. I had never even been out of England, except for a sortie or two into Southern Scotland and once to Wales for two days with a coach party.

'No, sir.'

For a moment I thought of Mike, but I knew he would be thrilled for me. He was an American student doing a year's course on Architecture at a college in London as part of his course from his University in Philadelphia. I had met him soon after my arrival in London, through my flat-mate. I knew Mike would want me to have a look at the U.S.A., even if it were a brief bird's eye view.

'See Miss Britton then. She'll advise you on clothing and extra expenses you're likely to incur. I take it your passport is in order?'

I flushed. 'I haven't one, sir.'

He frowned and looked impatient.

'You'd better arrange for that straight away. A visa. See to it.'

'Yes, sir.'

My life had taken on a dreamlike quality over the next week or two. Stella was a good ten years older than I and was used to quick trips of this kind. She had been to Iceland and Norway and more recently Spain. She was very competent, if as cool and detached as Dr. Manley. I was afraid of her too.

It was in Honolulu that I first saw some cracks in the armour of both of them, though it started with Stella, who developed a stomach upset. I thought she had been eating too much of the gorgeous pineapple, but her sickness was occurring in the mornings and it was soon easy to guess the cause. She was still called Miss Britton, but she had married Paul Sutton two years before, and she was as mad as a hornet at finding herself pregnant.

I saw little of Honolulu and might have thought the place a concrete jungle of high rise hotels surrounded by artificial grass and hundreds of shops, except that Dr. Manley took time off from dictating and left me to myself to explore, so that my impressions changed to lovely mountains, trees and flowers everywhere. And rain.

The rain heralded our departure for Malamba, which was a small island comparatively near, with unspoilt beaches, and in some places black sand. My impressions were beginning to be absorbed through a veil of exhaustion. Stella didn't feel or look well, and although Dr. Manley was not inhuman enough to reproach her, I could feel his impatience. I took on as much of her work as I could, as well as my own, but I could not help speculating about Elliot Manley, and wondering about his home and family background. I knew nothing about him whatsoever, and found Stella as close as an oyster when I ventured one or two leading questions. She was inclined to patronize me and let it be known that it was infra dig to ask questions.

But what a waste it all was . . . all that beauty and romance just waiting to be enjoyed. If only Mike had been with me!

Then the mood became grim and I forgot the islands in the sight of all the devastation wrought by the crash. The bodies had been identified and buried, but something had remained, and I shivered, feeling that over one hundred and fifty souls were still aimlessly wandering around, wondering why they had suddenly been thrown into the next world.

Stella and I remained at the hotel while Dr. Manley worked at the site. I took notes, typed reports and took notes again. Then, rather soberly, we were making the return flight with a relieved and rather subdued Stella resting as much as possible.

Back in London she felt unwell with blood pressure and had to give up her job, though I gathered she hoped it would be temporary until after her child was old enough to be looked after by someone else.

I got the job.

I also had a wonderful reunion with Mike. Betty Baxter, my flat-mate, went out and left us together, and we got carried away.

Mike couldn't marry me. There were all sorts of reasons why not, and we went over them many times. He was too young. He was on some sort of grant augmented by money from his parents who were not well off. There were rules and regulations to do with American citizenship.

'Forget it,' I said.

'Er . . . haven't your laws been altered to deal with cases like ours?' asked Mike, shamefacedly. 'Isn't it possible to have the baby . . . aborted?'

'I said forget it.'

No one was going to take my child away from me, even if it were born with only a twenty-year-old girl to depend on. I would manage somehow. I stared at Mike almost with dislike. What kind of man was he that he was willing to murder his own child?

'Berris . . . ' he said.

'I'll take care of it,' I told him, 'and myself. Just . . . just don't bother me any more.'

'But where will you go?'

'There are Homes for girls like me. Didn't you know?'

'Gee, Berris, I'm sorry . . . '

Suddenly he looked a mere boy, though he was a year older than I.

'It was my fault, too.'

'It was that night . . . seeing you again . . . talking about Hawaii . . . '

'I know. We lived it all again secondhand. I expect it would have happened if you had been with me on the trip just the same.'

I thought of Stella and smiled wryly. Wouldn't she laugh if she knew it was my turn now, only I wasn't like her. I didn't have a young T.V. executive like Paul Sutton working for me, and keeping me in comfort in a charming home. I only had a small cottage on the Cumbrian fells where the sheep got through the fence and ate the grass right up to the back door.

But it was somewhere to go.

* * *

I left it another two months before handing in my notice. I was thin to the point of being scraggy, and clever clothes disguised my ripening figure, though I could always plead too many fried meals in the evening. I tried to keep it from Betty, but she soon found out after I, too, had been sick in the mornings.

'My God, Berris,' she said. 'Is it Mike?'

'Who else?'

'What are you are going to do?'

'Leave me alone, Bet.'

'You absolute nit. Didn't you know a thing?'

'Oh, for God's sake, Bet, it just . . . just happened.'

'You know it'll be no good staying here. The landlord . . . '

'I know all about the landlord. You'll soon get another girl, Bet.'

She was kind and tried to comfort me.

'I like you, Berris. What are you going to do? Shall I write to my mum?'

'No! No . . . thanks, Bet. I'll be okay. I'll go home, that's all.'

'But you'll have nobody to look after you.'

'Let me worry about that.'

I had not thought much about actually handing in my resignation. It seemed one of the things of lesser importance, to be quickly done and quickly accepted.

But now Dr. Manley was gazing at me owl-like, then taking off his spectacles and polishing them, as though to see me the better. He looked so different without them that I was fascinated. He looked almost human.

'I would like a reason for your departure.'

'Personal reasons, sir.'

'Are you finding any aspect of the job here as my secretary uncongenial? In other words, Miss Martindale, do you find me difficult to work with?'

'Oh no, sir. Not at all. You've been very kind . . . very generous.'

He had. After Stella went he offered

me her job and immediately had my salary increased by a substantial amount. The thought of losing the job bit deeply. To think I had been mad enough to throw away so much. I refused to think I had ruined my life. I didn't happen to believe that to give life to another human being was so heinous that my own life was in ruins as a result. My child might be illegitimate, but who knows what the future would hold for it, or what it might do for humanity. Leonardo da Vinci had been illegitimate, hadn't he? . . . as had may great writers and composers. We would have been the poorer without them if their mothers had gone in for wholesale abortion.

'You've got an appointment with Mr. Swann, sir.'

'Who?'

'The representative of the Orbit Insurance Company. He's waiting now . . . '

He looked tired.

'We'll talk about this again, Miss Martindale. My secretaries seem to be leaving me in some numbers. I accept that, but I still like to know why. Miss Britton . . . or should I say Mrs. Sutton? . . . had an understandable excuse. But you . . .'

I felt the heat sticking my clothes to my back. Dr. Manley wasn't the most approachable of men. I shrank from the contempt in his eyes if he did find out. I could only repeat the mumble about personal reasons and beat a retreat.

I had not been too ashamed of what I had done, but Dr. Manley had a powerful effect on me, making me see my inadequacies and human failings sometimes for the first time with his cold direct gaze, and even with his more myopic one when he took off his spectacles as he seemed to do more and more these days. There had been no word of my replacement and I knew I would have to remind him as the days of my two weeks notice slipped past. I wanted to suggest Susan Crawley, but I shrank from this, knowing that it might invite another inquisition.

I thought up various excuses, none of which seemed to hold water, though already my mind was projecting itself into the future and the Cumbrian fells. I was a creature who often lived in the future, either because it beckoned more brightly, or because the present was unbearable.

Perhaps that's what made me believe the present was my secret which no one was likely to guess, so that it was all the more shocking when Dr. Manley asked me to stay behind to take a few notes. He had been working most of the day in the laboratory, and I knew he was lecturing to students the following day, so I found nothing unusual in this.

Most of the office staff had gone home except for the cleaners and caretaker, and I could hear their echoing footsteps in the corridor and their cheerful conversation as they threw down buckets and mops.

Dr. Manley was busy with his papers. I tested my ball point pen as I waited, my notebook at the ready. I had not been feeling too well for most of the day. If my situation had been normal, I would no doubt have been attending a Clinic by now for regular check-ups and tests for blood pressures, but I had not even been to see the doctor. There would be time enough for that when I got back to Highfield. Old Dr. Morville, who had looked after Aunt Grace so devotedly would no doubt look after me, too, even if he gave me a piece of his mind for being so foolish. But, the lecture over, he would soon soften up and I could be sure of expert care and attention. Meantime I was prepared to 'bite the blanket'.

I hoped Dr. Manley wouldn't need me for very long. He kept up a lively correspondence with, I gathered, an old friend from his University days who had taken up metal chasing and was now working in Copenhagen. They wrote highly technical letters to one another giving detailed accounts of work on which they happened to be engaged, and normally I found the letters absorbing to type, even though I could only grasp vaguely at the contents. I admired dedication, and the hours of study which both men put into their work, though my work as Dr. Manley's secretary, the bulk of which I had shouldered since I knew about the baby, only made me feel the more shallow and self-indulgent. I felt I had indulged in easy joy, quickly roused and quickly over, when there was so much I could have done to satisfy a different sort of hunger which was always in me. It has never occurred to me to envy girls who had studied hard at school and had been given the opportunity of a University career, but now I did. When they bore children, their trained minds would pass on that training, helping their child to develop mentally as well as physically. My child would be out of luck, except perhaps for love. I could supply that.

I was day-dreaming. It was something of a shock to find that Dr. Manley had cleared his desk and was now regarding me with the steady searching gaze which made me feel like a piece of burnt metal under his microscope.

'Sorry, sir. I'm quite ready.' I sat forward in my chair.

'Put that thing away . . . that notebook. I want to talk to you.'

I swallowed.

'Yes, sir.'

'I know a pregnant woman when I see one.'

I felt waves of sickness enveloping me, and a moment later he was round the desk and holding my shoulders, forcing my head forward. Then as I moved my body in protest, he went to a cupboard on the wall behind his desk and lifted out a bottle and two glasses, pouring out a small brandy with a gentle squirt of soda.

'Drink this.'

'I . . . ' I didn't like brandy. In fact, I didn't care for alcohol in any form.

'Drink it.'

I did, coughing a little. It warmed me and gradually I felt my body warming again as the room steadied round me.

'Now. Would you like to tell me about it?'

'No, sir.'

I avoided his eyes.

'How old are you, Miss Martindale?'

'Twenty, sir . . . and two months.'

'I take it you aren't secretly married? We have no rules here regarding the non-employment of married women.'

'No.'

'Is the man going to marry you?'

Suddenly I'd had enough. He was my employer, much older than I, and a man I respected beyond anyone I had ever met, but he had no right to question me. I stood up.

'I think that's my business, sir. I'd rather not talk about it.'

'Sit down.'

His voice was very quiet.

'I've given you my notice. I should like to leave quietly on Saturday, if you please. Miss Crawley could take over until . . . until you can find more staff.'

'Sit down . . . please.'

I sat down.

'Rightly or wrongly, I do feel a sense of responsibility towards you. Obviously you feel you can do without my help. I did have something to discuss . . . '

He was regarding me strangely, but I turned my head away, the colour flaming in my cheeks. What sort of person did he think I was? He had not been so concerned for Stella Sutton, but then, she'd been married hadn't she? Was I the first to leave under such a cloud? Surely other girls had faced such a problem alone?

'Very well. We'll leave it at that.'

Dr. Manley's usual brisk tone was back, his hands slapping the desk as he did after a pile of work had been dealt with.

I rose hurriedly.

'I can go, sir?'

'Yes.' He paused. 'Goodnight, Miss Martindale.'

'Goodnight sir.'

He wavered.

'If it's difficult for you to be here so

early in the mornings, you may arrive a little late if you wish. I shall expect you to telephone, however.'

I was unprepared for the rush of tears which made my voice thick and spongy. I could stand anything but his sympathy.

'Thank you, sir. I . . . I'll be fine.'

I had told Susan Crawley that I would be leaving, saying that I needed to go home to Cumbria. Office staff came and went, and I had never been communicative with the other girls. Susan was nice enough not to question me, though I saw her looking at me speculatively. Had she guessed, I wondered? If so, she was as tactful as she knew how. Dr. Manley would be better off with Susan than with me, I acknowledged rather forlornly. She was clever, competent and kind. He might even fall in love with her, if he didn't already have a glamorous wife installed at that address in Hampshire. I had found it among his other addresses. It was his home address, he had explained to me. He only used the flat in town during the week.

I was touched to find that the office staff had collected for a small parting gift, and it was significant that there was no good-humoured banter that it was not a wedding gift. They had played for safety and bought me a handbag in my favourite shade of brown, warm and rich. I had two pairs of shoes which would match exactly.

'Come and visit me at Highfield some time,' I said thoughtlessly to Susan, 'when you visit the Lake District. I'm quite near to Lake Bassenthwaite.'

'Thank you. That would be nice.'

Dr. Manley came to look for me and rather shyly I showed him the bag. He admired it coolly, and I felt rebuffed. It was as though he had never questioned me about my personal life, and was back to his coldly indifferent attitude. He handed me a cheque. I swallowed again when I saw that he had added a considerable bonus.

'If things become difficult you may contact me.'

'Thank you, sir.'

I never would. His tone was humiliating.

'Goodbye, Miss Martindale.'

He shook my hand.

'Goodbye, sir.'

I travelled home to Highfield the following Sunday.

I had written to Mrs. Shorrock, a neighbour who had been Aunt Grace's friend, and who had looked after the letting of the cottage for me. With the money from that added to Aunt Grace's small legacy and Dr. Manley's cheque, I would manage until after I had the baby. Living was cheaper at Highfield. I could get a few hens, milk from the farm, and there would be fruit and vegetables in the garden.

Betty had found another girl for the flat, though she promised to write. I knew she never would. She hated writing personal letters, even if she loved getting them, though they were thin on the ground.

'You'd receive more if you wrote a few yourself,' I had often told her.

Perhaps I would write to her now and again, but that, too, would fall away. There would be no point in holding on to the threads of my life in London.

Before making the journey north, I did a bit of shopping, buying some sensible clothing, a few books, some knitting wool and a toy rabbit for the baby. It was soft and fluffy with pink ears, and suddenly the thought of having a tiny daughter of my own was unbelievably precious. I was sure I would have a girl. For a brief spell I was happy, like a shaft of sunlight breaking through heavy clouds.

The books were on metals, Metal Techniques for Craftsmen, and I didn't know why I had bought them, except perhaps that they represented something I didn't want to lose entirely. Quite apart from my job, I had been interested in the subject for its own sake. I found it exciting that such wonderful materials with so many uses could be dug from the bowels of the earth. That, somehow, made man a rather wonderful creature in that he could manipulate and manufacture this bounty for the benefit of his fellow creatures. I had once tried to express these feelings to Dr. Manley and he had looked at me thoughtfully and given me one of his rare smiles.

'Man has had plenty of practice, Miss Martindale,' he said, gently. 'It's surely one of the oldest of our crafts.'

Unintentionally he had made me aware of the great gaps in my knowledge and as I knew there would be long hours at the cottage when I would have little else to do but contemplate the future for myself and my baby, I decided that if I merely learned how to spell some of the lesser known terms, it might be helpful towards getting a job again, though I was finding that it was wiser to live in the present these days, and to tell myself that I was still in my right mind and paying my way, and tomorrow was another day.

I had always loved my Cumbrian fells. Even in winter they were never cold and grey. The brilliant emerald and orange of dried bracken merely became muted, and the bare look of the trees only served to give them form and shape. Even on grey days the rain was refreshing, encouraging the growth of rich pastureland for the sheep which roamed freely over the fells and rested in small groups beside the mountain road.

Now, however, they did look dull and grey, though I knew the greyness was in myself. A tunnel of darkness lay ahead and as yet I could see no glimmer of light. I had written briefly to Mrs. Shorrock, a Lowland Scot by birth, though she had lived most of her life south of the Border. Her native accent was still strong, and sounded strange in my ears after the southern tongue.

'Have you been given a wee holiday?' she asked, after she welcomed me home to Highfield. 'You're looking well, if I may say so, Berris, though it's only in the body now I come to look at you. You're peelie-wallie about the face. It'll be the journey I don't doubt.'

'It was tiring.'

'I was going to write anyway, Berris my dear,' continued Mrs. Shorrock who was apt to go into long monologues. 'I made you a casserole, by the way, so that you could have it or not just when you arrived, or later if you wish. The tea's infused. I saw you from the side window. Yes. The bookings. Summer bookings. Some of last year's folk want to come back, Berris. They were suited, so they were. Fair suited. I thought you'd be pleased.'

I nodded, then felt ashamed. I would have to explain to Mrs. Shorrock that I wouldn't be letting this summer. I'd have to come to some sort of financial arrangement with her as well, since she got a percentage on all bookings, as well as being paid for looking after Highfield. Sooner or later she would have to be told that my 'bonny' appearance was not what it seemed. It was in the nature of a tribute that she had not viewed me with suspicion straight away.

However I wanted to settle in first, and rest a little before I put Mrs. Shorrock in the picture. I was in no doubt about what she would say since it was in her nature to be outspoken, but I preferred that to whispers behind one's back, or even to silent appraisal.

She said it all next day.

'I thought your Aunt Grace's teachings and good guidance would have counted for more, Berris. That's a fact. What were you thinking about to get yourself into a mess like this? What kind of man have ye got that would leave you to struggle through on your own?'

'I knew what I was doing, Mrs. Shorrock. Don't blame anybody else.'

'The more shame you then!'

'I'm paying the price myself, aren't I? Anyway, it's a baby I'm having, not a monkey.'

Her face softened.

'So you are, child. Your Aunt Grace would have upset herself, but she'd have stood by you. Poor lass, you needed your mother longer to keep you on the right road. You needed a firm hand. Anyway, I'll do all I can, lass. Have you got your wee things ready yet? Best get your bed booked, too . . . '

'Mrs. Shorrock, please . . . please leave it for a little while. There's time enough yet.'

'That's what we all think. Then it's as though there's no time at all. Where are you going?'

I was struggling into my anorak, and finding my boots.

'For a walk.'

'Not on the fells. You know fine it isn't the day. The mist can blow up and soak into you.'

'I haven't forgotten. I . . . I just need a walk.'

She was kind, but I needed to be on my own for a short while. Mrs. Shorrock always saw to my bodily comfort, but left me with no mental comfort whatsoever. I was home at Highfield, but unless I was very careful, I would find myself exploding with irritation.

2

My money was not going to last. I hadn't allowed for the thousand and one things a baby would need.

Dr. Morville gave me a wigging, but called once a week to take my blood pressure, which was up. Again I spared a thought for Stella.

'You'll have to rest,' he told me, 'or it's hospital for you, my lass.'

'Oh no!'

The thought of hospital made me sick, and I recalled the long hours in the spartan corridors when Aunt Grace was rushed there for a heart operation.

A small hotel in one of the nearby villages needed someone to do office work, and in spite of Dr. Morville's hoots of indignation, I applied for the job.

'It isn't strenuous,' I defended, 'and it will save me from worrying about myself. That's enough to send anyone's blood pressure up.'

Dr. Morville conceded that this might be so.

'You could do with . . . ' he paused, and I knew what he wanted to say because his eyes were angry again. Mike was getting more of the blame than I. 'You could do with somebody to look after you,' he finished.

'I could do with a fur coat as well.'

Spring can be capricious in my part of the country, sandwiching the odd fall of snow between days of blue skies and warm sunshine. I watched the lambs being born and the blackthorn making a bridal array of the hedgerows. I picked primroses and violets to relieve my depression, even as my body thickened and my hair grew lank for want of proper cutting.

But at least the fells looked glorious once again.

'There's a man down at Overwater asking the way to Highfield,' said Mrs. Shorrock, arriving breathless at the cottage one evening. 'He arrived this afternoon and Cathie Heald overheard him asking someone. She only got a quick look.'

'I'll bet!' Then the import of this news struck me. 'What did he look like?'

'A tall man. Dark.'

'Young?'

'Not so old.'

Mike? I hadn't told Mike about Highfield, and Betty wouldn't. She had promised. I hadn't wanted anything more to do with Mike. The baby was mine. I was paying for it, wasn't I? He wanted to go back to America, and the baby would only be a complication. He had hardly shown any great delight in the fact that he had fathered a child . . .

'Would it be your man?' asked Mrs. Shorrock, avidly.

'He is probably representing some new type baby food,' I told her.

She looked disappointed, believing me.

'Why come to you?'

'I sent away for a free sample of some new kind of disposable nappies. That's how they trace expectant mothers who are potential soft marks.'

'Oh.'

Who could it be? I wondered, uneasily. Would he turn up at the hotel where I was employed?

Mrs. Shorrock was looking out of the window.

'Land sakes, he's here,' she said. 'He's come in a posh car.'

'Owned by the firm I've no doubt.'

'Shall I stay and help you to get rid of him, Berris?'

'No thank you, I can do that myself. He'll be embarrassed at finding me on my own.'

I could see the vague outline of a man approaching the door, then the bell shrilled.

'Go the back way,' I said to Mrs. Shorrock. I didn't want her here if Mike had indeed come to find me, though who could have lent him the car? I could only see part of the bonnet as I made for the door.

It was Dr. Manley.

'Hello, Miss Martindale,' he greeted me. 'May I come in?'

I swallowed and retreated into the sittingroom. I could hear Mrs. Shorrocks rattling the doorlatch and pretending it was stiff.

'Do sit down, Dr. Manley,' I said clearly, though my legs were wobbling. 'I shall join you in a moment.'

I went through to the kitchen as the door was closing, then it opened again and Mrs. Shorrock's head appeared.

'Are you all right, Berris?'

'Perfectly all right. The gentleman is . . . was my employer. He probably needs my help over work I was doing.'

'Oh, I see.'

Her curiosity satisfied, I watched her going down the back path, then carried a bottle of sherry and a glass through to the sittingroom, and bent to light the log fire.

'Here, let me,' said Dr. Manley. 'You're . . . '

He looked uncomfortable and bent swiftly to light the paper and sticks.

'I'm out for most of the day,' I said. 'I do a clerical job at one of the hotels. Why have you come, Dr. Manley? Have I filed some important papers wrongly and caused havoc? No doubt you could have telephoned, but we never aspired to one, Aunt Grace and me.'

'You're very cut off.'

'It might appear so, but the grapevine is excellent. I already knew you were at Overwater and asking for directions here.'

He looked taken aback, then laughed.

'Bush telegraph, very good.'

Suddenly I laughed with him. It was astonishing, but I was so starved of company that I was glad to see him, though he was the last person I would have chosen to have paid me a visit.

'Do you have malted milk or something?' he asked, taking the sherry. 'I remember you don't drink alcohol.'

What a surprising memory the man had for details!

‘Have you decided on a walking holiday perhaps?’

‘No. I came to see you.’

I could no longer hide my astonishment. He was as coldly impersonal as ever, and it was completely out of character for him to worry about an employee in my situation. He had already done more than enough for me.

‘But . . . Why?’

He was silent, staring at me.

‘I find it hard to explain, or begin to explain. I came to put a proposition to you.’

‘You know I can’t accept propositions at the moment. I . . . I intend to keep my child.’

‘I know. That helps. All right, I’ll come straight to the point. I’ve come to ask you to marry me.’

I felt as though I had touched a live electric cable.

‘You . . . you . . . ’

He held up a hand.

‘Please . . . hear me out. I’m in a difficult . . . very difficult situation. My sister has been in hospital after an accident and she's now ready to come home. I need someone to look after her, someone I can trust . . . someone who will stay until my sister is better. In return I'll give you a home and your child a name.'

I was so astonished I could hardly speak.

'I've never heard anything so . . . ' I couldn't find words. 'You want to *marry* me, just so that I'll look after your sister . . . '

His colour was high.

'Surely you aren't in love with me?'

The Dr. Manley I knew well suddenly stared at me.

'Of course not, Miss Martindale.'

'But suppose you fall in love with someone . . . I mean . . . '

'I had already decided never to marry.' His voice was like ice.

'Then I'm completely bewildered.'

He got up to gaze out of my tiny cottage window.

'Maybe it was a preposterous idea as

you so clearly imagine. Let's say no more about it.'

Suddenly I had the odd feeling that he was the one who needed help.

'Look, if it were practical or could be arranged, I would gladly come and look after your sister. There would be no need to . . . to go to such lengths.'

I had never really understood him, I thought, looking at him curiously. I had thought him a cold, competent, rather ruthless machine, utterly without feelings except for what he considered his duty. Was he so wrapped up in his work that he didn't live in a normal world? Was the real key to his character the fact that he was supremely naïf. Was he . . . even . . . a little odd?

Then I saw that I was wrong as he turned round. He was ruthless all right, but he was also clever and practical.

'No, Miss Martindale, the matter is more . . . more delicate than I would care to discuss unless you're more interested than you obviously are. My sister needs very special care, such as only someone close to her could give. Her nerves are very bad. Her husband is still in hospital as a result of the same accident, and likely to be there for some time. I need someone with more authority than a nurse or a housekeeper. I already have a housekeeper, and she knows her place. I must confess I thought of you because you may have as much to gain as to lose by the arrangement. You could have a home, a background for your child and every protection. In return you would have to devote a great deal of time to Dympna. It would not be easy. Later . . . when she's better . . .' he shrugged.

Dympna. Hearing her name, she seemed to take on flesh and blood. What sort of woman was she that he was willing to saddle himself with a wife he didn't love, not to mention a child, just to have her looked after? Though obviously he thought divorce would be easy.

He must have seen the continuing doubt in my eyes, and all the questions he didn't want to answer unless I had shown myself eager to leap at his proposal. A few years ago a woman in my position *would* have leapt at it, and would have been on her knees thanking God for the opportunity. But now . . . were things so very different? Wouldn't my child have a much better chance in life under Elliott Manley's protection?

'I can see that a wife might be a help in the circumstances,' I said, slowly, 'but a child . . .'

'I like children.'

Then why had he already decided not to marry, until now? And why was he only offering his name and his protection?

'You only know one parent of this child.'

'Perhaps.'

'I would like to think it over,' I said, slowly. 'It's much too big an issue to be decided immediately.'

'Very well.' He hesitated. 'What are your plans? Can you have lunch with me at the hotel?'

'I have a job to do.'

'Is it so important?'

'At the moment, yes . . . until I've thought about . . . things.'

'I'll come and see you tomorrow evening.'

He was completely impersonal and might have been interviewing me again as the office junior.

'Very well, Dr . . . ' I stopped, thinking how incongruous it was that I could only call him 'Dr. Manley'. We would have made excellent Victorians!

I had expected a sleepless night, but on the contrary I slept better than I had done for weeks, as though my burden was already being lightened a little. Next day I was unwell again, and felt the strain of holding down my job while trying also to hold down my blood pressure.

Long before I arrived back home, I knew that whatever the distant future held for me, the immediate future held a solution too tempting to ignore.

As I travelled back from my job in the late afternoon, sitting slumped in the front seat of our small local bus, I stared out at the fields, freshly green after rain rapidly clearing under shafts of sunshine which were making a double rainbow over the fells. The hoop of one rainbow dropped over the locality where Dr. Manley was staying. Perhaps he was my crock of gold, I thought, though I wasn't thinking of riches. Gold could mean things other than money.

There were sheep and young lambs on the mountain road. The farmers had had a good lambing season. Invariably there were losses and other sheep had to foster some of the lambs, but after initial effort it was fairly easy to get a sheep to accept a lamb not its own. My own child would be born in about three months time and, looking at the animals contented and secure in their familiar surroundings, I thought again of Dr. Manley. Would he really care about my child, or would he come to hate us after his sister was better? Obviously he thought separation would be easy, but by then I would have given up my independence. I was fighting to be strong now. If I let it all go, wouldn't it be all the more difficult later?

I almost forgot to get out of the bus at Highfield, but the driver knew where everybody lived. He made some jovial remarks about daydreaming and I smiled briefly, hating to see the kindness and sympathy in his eyes. It was the small things which hurt.

* * *

By the time Dr. Manley arrived at Highfield that evening, I had made up my mind to accept his proposal. I had done a lot of thinking and I knew that my greatest hesitation had been because of a sense of inadequacy. I was in awe of him, and respected him more than anyone I knew. It had seemed incongurous that someone like me, who was no one, should be his wife. My mother had been a hill farmer's daughter, married to an artist whose erratic career had hardly been the basis for security. *She* had provided that, while he drank at local inns and painted pictures which he had sold for a few pence. I had only one left, a portrait he painted of my mother which her sister, my Aunt Grace, had kept for me.

Recently I heard rumours that Marcus Martindale pictures were bringing in much bigger sums, but it was rather too late for me, and I doubted if they were good enough to give me prestige enough to feel equal to Dr. Manley. Besides they were my father's contribution to the world, not mine.

But now something, the proposal of marriage itself perhaps, was giving me a new pride in myself. I was young, but there was potential in me . . . or so I thought. I would improve.

When Dr. Manley arrived, I had prepared a small supper and I was wearing my one good dress which still fitted. I had also found time to wash and dry my hair, the one feature I had inherited from my father. Aunt Grace used to say it was his dark auburn hair which had attracted my mother to him in the first place.

When I opened the door to him, Dr. Manley looked pale, his dark eyes tired behind those owl-like spectacles. His manner didn't soften when he saw my preparations. He turned to stare at me, his eyes flickering over the long dress and, I hoped, my well-brushed hair. He could hardly fail to guess which way my mind had been made up, but he looked anything but pleased by my decision.

I was never the one for shilly-shallying, and he looked far from being a prospective bridegroom.

'You can see that I had made up my mind to accept your offer,' I told him, sitting down, 'but I suspect you're regretting that you've made it. Am I right?'

He looked taken aback, then his eyes gleamed.

'I'd forgotten that you have a habit of coming straight to the point. Miss Mar . . . Berris. Berris.' He repeated my name. 'Yes, I had changed my mind. I had forgotten till I saw you again how . . . how young you are. I was asking far too much of you. The human mind searches in strange channels for solutions to seemingly insoluble problems.'

He couldn't know how disappointed I felt. He would never know. Briefly I had glimpsed something wonderful, but now it had gone.

'I don't blame you,' I said. 'I'm no catch for anyone. I thought I could be for a little while. You can see my background. This is all I have. My mother's people owned a farm, but it has changed hands long since. My father was an artist, Marcus Martindale. Now other people make money selling his pictures. All I would have to offer would be someone else's child.'

I hadn't intended to sound bitter, but I must have done. Dr. Manley leaned forward and took my hand, though I kept my arm rigid, wanting to repel him.

'I'm thinking of you. You're young. You've made a mistake, but you'll get over that and you'll marry someone you can love . . . someone young. I'm . . . rather old . . . '

I looked a him.

'Thirty-nine', he said.

'I don't call that old!'

'Sometimes . . . ' he stopped. 'I couldn't offer you the sort of love you deserve. I was only offering . . . responsibility.'

'Looking after your sister.'

'Yes. A very special sister.'

'You love her?'

He didn't reply for a moment. 'She's special because she's being discharged from a . . . a special sort of hospital. They think it will help her to come home.'

I stared at him incomprehendingly. I could hear the loud ticking of my wallclock, then the beating of my heart.

'Her husband is still in hospital. He's

a charming person, a college lecturer. It was a car accident, and Dympna was driving.'

'But . . . but surely . . . '

'She drove towards a wall. Deliberately. She tried to kill Gerald and herself. She . . . she hasn't been herself.'

'You mean she . . . she's mentally ill.'

'It was a temporary thing.' He was trying to convince himself. I knew that. 'She's very quiet now. The authorities think she's well enough now, with . . . with proper care and an interest in life. You could give her that . . . and the child . . . '

At last I was getting the picture, and I felt sick. I had thought he was willing to marry me in spite of the child, but now it seemed that he had thought of me *because* of it.

'I see.'

Suddenly I remembered the casserole I had made, and I could smell it in the oven.

'Excuse me . . . '

I bounded to my feet and hurried into the kitchen. One does odd things when one's mind is faced with more than it can take. Mine sought refuge in the ordinary.

'It smells good.'

Dr. Manley had followed me, staring at the bubbling casserole as I removed the lid. I was no longer hungry, but perhaps he was.

'Would you like some?'

'Why not? Perhaps we'll both feel better. Here. Let me.'

He carried it through to the table, then lit the candles. 'This is nice.'

I choked back the tears. I had meant it as a celebration, not a stopgap to misery and despair. I had been reconciled to my lot before Dr. Manley came along, upsetting me. Now I felt I couldn't face what lay ahead. He had, very briefly, taken the load and now that he had handed it back, I felt crushed.

'Go on. Eat up. My guess is that you haven't eaten much today. If it's any consolation, neither have I.'

I ate a little. It was good. Aunt Grace had taught me to use local herbs in my cooking, and I knew I could hold my own in that direction with anyone.

'This is delicious,' Dr. Manley was saying, but I was crying right there into my casserole, great tearing sobs full of the desolation I felt.

'I'll be okay. Sorry about that,' I said, as I saw that he was wondering how to comfort me.

'What are you going to do?'

It was none of his business . . . now!

'Take care of myself of course. What are *you* going to do?'

We stared at one another.

'I don't know. Get a nurse, if I can. Hope Dympna will feel better in time. Hope Gerald will be well enough one day to leave hospital and they can take up the threads of their life again. He doesn't blame her, though she probably blames herself. That's why it . . . it will take a little time.'

'Is he very badly injured?'

'He's had several operations. Eventually he will be well again.'

'Is your only reservation because you feel it isn't fair to me?'

'Yes. It wouldn't be fair.'

'After your sister is quite better, and I too am on my feet, we could get a divorce, couldn't we? Especially . . . '

'An annulment, perhaps?'

'Yes.'

'It is possible.'

'Then if you ask me again, I'll accept. You were right. I would have more to gain than to lose, and I'd be happy to look after your sister.'

Once again I could hear the clock ticking away the minutes of my life.

'I'm asking you,' he said, very quietly. 'Are you willing to marry me, Berris?'

'Yes.'

It was a moment caught in time. I had no means of knowing then, just what I had taken on.

3

When he set eyes on our small village Church where I had been christened, Elliott insisted on a proper wedding even though it might be of short duration. My parents were buried in the Churchyard there, and the Vicar called regularly, and had not lectured me when he found out about my baby.

'We'll have the banns called properly, and you can prepare for a simple wedding . . .'

'White gown,' I said, rather bitterly, and his face hardened.

'Don't be stupid. I'm trying to do what is best for you, and if you can't see that . . .'

'I'm sorry,' I said, humbly.

He was full of surprises, was my husband-to-be. I could see he was giving me a sense of security by arranging the sort of wedding I would have had if I had not messed up my life. He was wise enough to know that the kind of marriage he was offering would hardly give me that sense of security, unless he arranged it this way.

'I've got to go back to London, but I'll arrange as much as I can before I go. I take it you'll only want a few friends, even if we are being married in Church?'

'Quite correct. Mrs. Shorrock and her husband, I suppose. I can't think who else . . .'

'Er . . . I'll leave you a cheque since you'll want some clothes . . .

'No Dr. Manley . . . Elliott . . . please don't do that. I . . . I have a little money. I'll supply my own wedding dress. After that . . . after that it will be different. I'll be earning my keep, as it were.'

He looked at me uncertainly, then shrugged.

'All right, we won't argue over trifles. Now, we'd better consult your old Vicar and set a date for the wedding.'

In the end quite a few people turned up at the Church, and I was showered with confetti and rose petals. Dr. and Mrs. Morville had agreed to be our witnesses, though I had a quiet talk with Dr. Morville, telling him a little of what had happened so that he would not start having dour thoughts with regard to Elliott. We went back to the cottage where Mrs. Shorrock had insisted on doing the wedding breakfast, then we left everything in her capable hands, as Elliott carried my few possessions, packed in two suitcases, out to the car and deposited them in the boot.

Amidst congratulations I was helped into Elliott's comfortable car and as we drove away, I turned to take another look at Highfield, little realising in what circumstances I would see it again. Suddenly I wanted to go back, to shelter within its familiar walls, and crouch before the log fire in the kitchen. I was being winkled out of its sheltering protection and being made to face the world again, in an entirely new life, when I just wanted to hide away and be quiet. Nervous fears made me shiver and Elliott put out a hand and grasped my fingers.

'Cold, Berris?' he asked. 'The heater will soon warm up.'

'It's nerves,' I told him honestly. 'I'll soon be okay.'

'I know how you feel.'

Suddenly I realised that it must be equally difficult for him. He had worries ahead about which I seemed to know very little.

'Where are we going?' I asked.

'London first of all, to my flat. Then after I attend to a few things there, we'll go to Rosenwell, my home in Hampshire, where you will meet my housekeeper, Mrs. Sutton. Before leaving London, we will go to Newlands . . . a nursing home in the Northern outskirts, and you can meet Gerald, my brother-in-law. I'd like you to get to know him before . . . before you meet Dympna.'

'I see.'

Again I shivered. They were all just names, but soon they would be people close to me. The shining new wedding ring on my left hand had made them relatives . . . Gerald . . . Dympna . . . even Mrs. Sutton . . . Suppose I could make no contact with any of them. I would just succeed in complicating Elliott's life even more.

I glanced at him, feeling oddly proud that he was my husband. He was handsome and distinguished, and very well-groomed, very different from Mike and the other young men I used to know.

We were driving towards Scotch Corner, and the M1 Motorway.

'We'd better stay at a Hotel overnight,' said Elliott, looking at his watch. 'It's been too big a day to drive all the way to London, and it would tire you out.' He was silent for a moment. 'Don't worry, you'll have your own room.'

I said nothing, being reminded once

again that I was really only an extra housekeeper on his staff, even if I was one with special status. That had been necessary to assist me in doing my job.

'Very well,' I managed, evenly, and shivered again.

'Tomorrow we buy you a heavier coat,' said Elliott, rather grimly. 'I can't have you catching a chill.'

He could not add to his worries in other words. I made no protest, but I knew that no overcoat would be warm enough to melt the ice inside my body. I wondered if I would ever really be warm again.

I had thought I would have little appetite for the dinner we had at a small quiet hotel later that evening. I had been too excited to eat very much of Mrs. Shorrock's daintily served wedding breakfast, and now I felt too tired to study the menu closely, but Elliott ordered for both of us, and soon I was eating with reasonable appetite.

It was a nice hotel, quiet and homely instead of the large expensive five-star

I had expected Elliott to choose. Again I was touched by his thoughtfulness, though I lay awake for a long time in the comfortable bed, watching the shadows flicker as traffic passed by on the Motorway, some distance away, and listening to the faint hum of cars and lorries, finding it oddly soothing. There were dozens of people, still in their cars, bent on travelling to or from business affairs, or perhaps hurrying to reach a loved one who had taken ill, or even trying to flee from a life which was ensnaring them. There might be quite a number of them with problems greater than mine. Many might think me lucky if they knew my situation, and compared it with their own.

I sighed and rolled over to a more comfortable position. I was small-boned and thin, and my pregnancy was as yet not too cumbersome, but I had often to find a good relaxed position before falling asleep. I caressed the new shining wedding ring. It was all I had to show that my life was any different tonight from the previous night.

A silent tear tickled my ear, and I let it stay wet on my cheek, but it was as much for Elliott Manley as for myself. He was not exactly getting a good deal out of our arrangement either.

We reached North London early the following afternoon, and Elliott left the Motorway and began to drive along quiet roads, passing through pretty villages so different from the villages back home, yet each had their own charm for me.

'Where are we going?' I asked.

'I thought I had mentioned it,' said Elliott. 'I would like you to meet Gerald, my brother-in-law. I thought you ought to meet him before we see Dympna. It . . . it might help you to understand her . . . or understand why I'm concerned for her. Gerald has been my friend for a number of years. He's a quiet, scholarly man. I think you'll like him.'

We passed through a village named

Merrendon, and turned into a tree-lined driveway between two old stone pillars. There were two notices, one which said that it was a private road, and the other 'Merrendon Hall Nursing Home.'

Elliott seemed to be well-known by the Staff, and we were shown into a quiet but well-furnished room occupied by the Matron, a tall slender lady who seemed to go with the room. Elliott introduced me as his wife, and I felt her keen eyes on me. She must have been eaten up with curiosity that I, obviously younger than Elliott and expecting a child, had not yet met my brother-in-law, Gerald Moryson.

Perhaps that accounted for the reserve I could sense in her manner as she discussed her patient with Elliott.

'Mr. Moryson is making excellent progress,' she said, 'though it will be many weeks yet before he will be back to health. The form of injury he received in the accident is one of the most difficult to predict how he will react. I've seen people recover very quickly and respond well to physiotherapy, but others have to use a wheelchair for quite a few months, then use walking aids. But Mr. Moryson . . . he's a good patient . . . he wants to get better.'

I could feel that she wanted to say a great deal more, but hardly knew how to discuss this. Perhaps that was due to my presence, and no doubt Elliott had already discussed his brother-in-law's case at length with doctors, specialists, surgeons and anyone else he thought would be able to help, as well as the Matron. I was beginning to grasp how much Elliott wanted to see Gerald Moryson well again, not only for his own sake but for his sister's, who had caused the accident.

The Matron conducted us to a lovely room with a view overlooking the park. At one time a wealthy family must have lived here, and no doubt they'd had the grounds skilfully landscaped to enhance the beauty of their property. Now the

Hall was an obviously expensive nursing home, and I knew that Elliott would be footing the bill for the care of his brother-in-law.

I walked round the door of the room, feeling horribly embarrassed, but understandably curious, and as Elliott led me forward and introduced me, I felt an odd sensation as though I had been subjected to an intense scrutiny, then dismissed as valueless. It was surely only my own nerves, however, as I found myself shaking hands with the most noble-looking man I had ever seen. He had beautiful snow-white hair and the face of a saint, his brown eyes soft and gentle, and a smile of welcome showing beautifully even white teeth. His features were classically handsome and I could sense the respect and affection the two men felt for one another.

'I . . . I haven't told you about Berris before,' Elliott was saying, rather awkwardly. 'You were too ill. She's been living at her home up North, but I'm bringing her to Rosenwell. She'll be there, when Dympna comes home.'

I thought I saw the flicker of a nerve at the corner of Gerald's eyes when his wife's name was mentioned, but a short time later I decided I must have been mistaken. There was no change in the gentleness of his expression.

'My poor Dympna,' he said, shaking his head. 'She'll be blaming herself for something which was an accident. Did you tell her, Elliott, that she must not blame herself?'

Elliott's face had gone rather hard and white.

'We haven't been able to discuss it, Gerald. I . . . I may be able to talk to her after she comes home.'

We did not stay long, much to my relief. I had found little to say to Gerald Moryson, feeling that there was an incredible gap between us. He was a scholar and a philosopher, and my husband's great friend as well as brother-in-law. Beside him I felt smaller than ever. Beside him, I was nothing.

Yet he had the kindness to take my hand.

'Elliott never ceases to surprise me,' he said, quietly. 'I had no idea he was contemplating marriage, so you must give me time to get used to having a sister-in-law. I must say that some of his surprises are very nice indeed.'

Elliott was looking rather uncomfortable and Gerald immediately put it down to the fact that we had little time to spare.

'I'll be back soon, I promise,' said Elliott. 'Keep your spirits up. Anything you need?'

'Nothing. You've thought of everything. I . . . I appreciate the time you have given me when . . . when I know how valuable it is to you.'

'I'll try to spare more, I promise,' said Elliott again.

Together we walked out to the car, and Elliott drove away, rather raggedly, though he quickly settled down to normal driving.

'Honestly, there's no one like

Gerald,' he said. 'He never complains about Dympna, yet how . . . how frustrated he must feel. She doesn't deserve the love he has for her.'

I said nothing. I didn't know enough about it, and I wasn't at all sure how I felt about Gerald which was making me feel strangely disquieted. How awful it would be if I didn't like Elliott's only relations!

'You're very quiet. Are you tired? Has it all been too much for you?'

Elliott's voice was suddenly gentle and kind, so that I had a ridiculous desire to weep all over again. My voice sounded almost brusque in an effort to keep away the tears, though I hardly knew why I was crying, except that somewhere that old sense of shame was with me again.

'I'm all right,' I said.

'We'll go straight to my flat and you can rest while I go into the office and attend to accumulated business. You can rest there until I've cleared things up, then I'll take you to Rosenwell. I have a housekeeper, Mrs. Sutton, who will take care of you till you settle in.'

Suddenly the tears would no longer stay away, and I felt for my handkerchief.

'There are man-sized tissues behind you,' said Elliott rather impersonally. 'It would upset you, seeing Gerald like that, but it had to be done. In order to be of any help to Dympna, you must get to know both of them. We'll have a meal at the flat, then you'll begin to feel better, and it's a service flat, as you know. You need do nothing but rest for the next two days, and perhaps do some shopping for yourself and . . . and . . . clothes and things.'

I knew what he meant, but I would buy nothing for my baby with Elliott's money until I had earned it. Already I had quite a decent layette in one of the cases, thanks to my job at Highfield.

'You must get a heavy coat,' Elliott insisted, and I managed to smile and accept that with good grace. I needed a good heavy coat, but in return I would see that Elliott got the best value for his money that I could give him. I would look after Dympna like a children's nanny with her most precious charge.

Beyond that I could not see, but I was determined to do my best.

Three days later we travelled to Rosenwell, Elliott's beautiful home in Hampshire. He must have already told Mrs. Sutton, his housekeeper, a little about me because she showed no surprise when she came forward to greet us as Elliott escorted me up the wide steps, and into a large square hall. The heavy oak door had been standing open and Mrs. Sutton obviously looking for our arrival, since she hurried forward so promptly, giving me a keen glance. I had no idea whether she approved of what she saw or not.

I had already been rather demoralized by the sight of the house which seemed to be of enormous proportions after my little cottage at Highfield. I had been too conscious of the vast number of windows, all staring at me, to appreciate the true beauty of the place . . . that was to come later . . . and now I felt that I was in grave danger of regarding Mrs. Sutton as another Mrs. Danvers!

'This is my wife,' said Elliott, introducing us, and the older woman shook hands with just the right degree of firmness.

'It is good to welcome a new Mrs. Manley,' she said. 'It's a number of years now since the Mistress died . . . '

'Mrs. Sutton has been with us a great many years,' said Elliott. 'I hope you've got something nice cooking for dinner, Sutty, such as lamb pie.'

She smiled, looking suddenly human. 'And apple pancakes, Mr. Elliott.'

'Very fattening,' said Elliott, turning to me. 'Build you up, Berris dear.'

It was the first time he had used any endearment when speaking to me, so that I felt my cheeks redden, then remembered that it would be expected of him in front of Mrs. Sutton. She must already be eaten up with curiosity about me, seeing that I was going to have a child, and I thought she was casting a few disapproving glances in Elliott's direction as she said she would escort me up to our rooms, since I must be tired.

I was introduced to John Makin and his wife, Ena, who lived in the gardener's cottage and helped out in the house. They had a daughter, Rose, who was due to leave school, and who later became a great help and comfort to me, in the difficult months which were to lie ahead.

John Makin carried in our cases and I followed Mrs. Sutton upstairs, and along a wide corridor lined with pictures, though bright with magnolia walls and white paintwork, the carpet soft shades of blue and gold, to a large room overlooking the front of the house. There was a fire burning brightly in the grate, and the whole room had a welcoming air, though I viewed the large double bed with a pang of doubt. Was the room meant to be shared with

Elliott? . . . or was it mine alone? Somehow I had the feeling that it was the master bedroom.

'I've arranged things rather hurriedly, madam,' said Mrs. Sutton. 'Mr. Elliott rather . . . er . . . sprung the fact that he was married on to us . . .'

I had turned away, the heat of the room not helping my embarrassed blushes, but I managed to control my inward shaking.

'That's all right, Mrs. Sutton,' I said, evenly. 'It could not be nicer.'

'This door leads to the dressing room, and the bathroom is here. Mr. Elliott said you had not been well, which was why he left you in your old home for a while, but I'm sure you will wish to settle in now . . . ' She trailed off, but I didn't help her.

'Of course.'

'I'll run a bath for you, and there's a warm house-dress belonging to Miss Dympna which might be better than airing off your own clothes for this evening. Miss Dympna used to like to wear that dress after she had travelled home from a long journey . . .'

'No thanks, I'll wear my own,' I told her. 'I . . . I have a warm dress in that blue case which will do. We will leave Miss Dympna's things untouched till she comes home.'

I did not want to wear another girl's clothes. I had still to meet Dympna Moryson, and felt that it would be an imposition to accept the use of any of her garments till we had met, and had sized one another up! I felt, too, that I must show Mrs. Sutton that I had a mind of my own, and preferred to make my own decisions, and she seemed to take this point as she nodded and removed my new warm woollen coat, hanging it away in the wardrobe.

Elliott had gone into his study to go through the mail, and I had already bathed and changed when he came upstairs to look for me. My clothes had been unpacked and hung away, though I had asked Mrs. Sutton to leave the case in which I had packed the baby clothes. I would see to that one myself.

'Comfortable, Berris?' Elliott asked, as I finished brushing my hair. The long blue wool gown I wore was no doubt a poor thing compared with Dympna's, but it felt fresh and comfortable, and my cheeks glowed after my bath.

'Very comfortable, except that . . . Elliott . . . couldn't I have that other bedroom? . . . the one Mrs. Sutton called the dressing room?'

'That's mine,' said Elliott. 'I have explained to Mrs. Sutton. This bedroom is entirely your own till . . . till after the child is born. You can come up here and be alone, if you wish, at any time. There's a small bureau where you can write, and books to read, though you will find a well-stocked library downstairs. Or you may just wish to rest on that couch.'

'Oh Elliott . . . I hardly know what to say.'

Once again I felt the poignancy of our situation as I saw the look of sadness in his eyes.

'Don't worry, you'll earn it . . . when Dympna comes home,' he told me. 'Relax all you can until then.'

* * *

The following day Mrs. Sutton showed me over the house which proved to be smaller than I had thought from first impressions. The old stables, now used as garages, were all incorporated in the main building, together with a wood shed and storage barn which contained the central heating tank.

The house had six bedrooms and two bathrooms, with four spacious downstairs rooms and a larger modern kitchen.

'It used to be several small rooms, such as a scullery and butler's pantry, as well as a kitchen,' Mrs. Sutton told me, 'but Mr. Elliott had it modernized when . . . when he asked me to come back.'

'You've been away?'

'Yes. I got married. Mrs. Knight was

housekeeper here in old Mrs. Manley's day, but she's retired now. Then when Miss Dympna got married, and I was widowed, I came back to Rosenwell. Mrs. Manley was a lovely lady . . . Irish, you know. Mr. Manley wasn't here very much. He was away on business a lot.'

I would like to have heard all I could about Elliott's family, but something inside was finding distaste in gossiping with Mrs. Sutton. I found that I liked her, but I could sense the uncertainty in her as she looked at me, and I knew she was longing to ask a thousand questions, so I stuck to general things and asked questions about the household needs instead. I learned that the cupboards were stacked with enough linen, silver, china and pottery to last the next fifty years.

Mrs. Sutton did all the marketing and planned the meals. The house was easy to clean being well cared for by Ena Makin over the years. The lounge was a huge room with a large open fireplace and a basket stacked with logs in one corner. The deep Chesterfields were chintz-covered, and the walls were painted white and covered with pictures. I viewed these with delight, thinking that something of my father's love of Art had been passed on to me. There was a huge grand piano which I looked at admiringly, and Mrs. Sutton ran a gentle finger over its polished surface.

'Miss Dympna was the one to play the piano,' she said.

'Was? I'm sure she'll play it again,' I said, rather sharply. She spoke as though Elliott's sister was dead, along with her parents.

'Yes, of course. Er . . . is there word of her coming home then?'

I bit my lip. Obviously Elliott had not discussed Dympna's home-coming with the housekeeper.

'I can't tell you when she'll be coming home,' I said, with truth.

'Well, I'm glad you're here to be with her, madam,' she said, and I knew she meant every word. I could sense the relief in her, and once again I felt a twinge of apprehension. What would Dympna Moryson be like? Would I be able to control her, if she had violent impulses now and again? Suppose she turned violent when Elliott was away from home in some other part of the world, where his expert knowledge was needed?

We had gone into the diningroom, where the long mahogany table shone with polish. The carpet and curtains were sapphire blue, and I could imagine that at one time many elegant dinner parties would have been given here by the Manleys.

Next to the diningroom was a small cosy room with a television. The chairs were old and shabby, but very comfortable.

'This was Mrs. Manley's sewing room,' said Mrs. Sutton, 'and Miss Dympna used it for general relaxation.'

'I think I'd like to do the same, Mrs. Sutton,' I said, looking round with pleasure. It reminded me of Highfield, with its shabby carpet, and cosy fireplace, where a fire had been set.

Across the hall was Elliott's study, and he came to the door when he heard our voices, inviting me to look round while he asked Mrs. Sutton to bring us coffee. He had obviously been getting through a lot of work.

'Has Mrs. Sutton shown you everything, Berris dear?' he asked. 'I just wanted you to get the general lay-out with regard to running the house, but later I'll show you round, and tell you a little about the pictures and the furniture.'

'It's all beautiful, Elliott,' I said, sincerely. 'It seems a shame . . .'

I broke off, embarrassed. I had been going to say that it seemed a shame not to have a mistress of the house looking after it all, and bringing the house to life again since it all seemed to be waiting for something to happen.

Then I remembered that *I* was the new mistress, and all that was going to happen was that I would have my child here, and it would not be a Manley. And that the waiting was for Elliott's sister who was too sick to give the house what it needed. I could see it filled with agreeable company, and happy laughter, instead of this quiet but rather dead beauty.

'What's a shame?' he was asking. 'Not to use it to the full?'

I nodded and he turned to gaze at me.

'What would that mean?'

'Oh . . . just people being happy.'

He turned away.

'It seems a long time since it was full of people being happy. Do you think you can find happiness here, Berris?'

'I . . . I think so.'

'Then perhaps that would be a start, my dear.'

Mrs. Sutton wheeled in a trolley with a large pot of coffee, fine china cups, and a bowl of biscuits with a large fruit cake. Elliott cut a huge slice of the fruit cake for himself, after I decided I had better stick to eating a small savoury biscuit. The coffee was delicious, and suddenly I felt a glow of well-being. This was Rosenwell and for the time being, at least, I was the mistress of the house, and I felt a glow of fierce pride, as I looked round Elliott's study which doubled as a library, with shelves full of books.

'Shall I be able to read them?' I asked, shyly.

'Any you want. They've been catalogued. You like books, Berris?'

I nodded. 'Do you want me to help with your correspondence?'

He hesitated, then shook his head.

'No. I'm nearly up to date. Most of it will be done at the office, anyhow. No . . . just get to know Rosenwell before my sister comes home. Try to feel that it's your home, Berris.'

I nodded, glancing out of the window at the wide expanse of lawns where John Makin was cutting the grass with a sit-on mower. The sight of the gardener going about his work reminded me that it was not really my world, so that suddenly I felt a stranger again.

'I'll work till lunch-time, then we'll have a walk around the gardens. I must leave for London by four o'clock.'

'Shall I be going with you?' I asked, eagerly . . . too eagerly . . . so that Elliott frowned.

'No, it's best you stay here,' he said. 'As I say, try to get to know the place, and to get used to running it. Mrs. Sutton is very capable and will help you, I'm sure.'

I nodded, but I wondered how I could ever help Mrs. Sutton!

4

The following week was the longest I had spent since the first week of my return home to Highfield. After the first few days of trying to work with Mrs. Sutton, I let her go her own competent way, and spent my time wandering around the grounds of Rosenwell, then in and out of the rooms when the weather broke and it rained heavily. Mrs. Sutton lit the fire for me in the small snug morning room, which I began to feel was my own. She had her own quarters in the house, but I invited her to keep me company one evening, and asked her, casually, if she knew Gerald Moryson, Dympna's husband. Mrs. Sutton's eyes glowed, and she told me what a charming and thoughtful man he was.

'Miss Dympna never seemed to appreciate him,' she said. 'She was a happy enough girl growing up, but after she married Mr. Gerald, she seemed to change. Of course he's a handsome man, and I often wondered if she wasn't jealous of him. Not that there was any need. He was devoted to her. You could see it in so many ways, yet she seemed to take all of it without so much as a word of thanks. I think it upset Mr. Elliott, since he and Mr. Gerald were such friends. Then she goes and crashes her car . . . all nerved up she'd be, though it hurt Mr. Gerald as well as herself. I'm glad you're here, madam, to be with her when she comes home. You'll be company for her, and maybe that's what she needs . . . young company.'

Elliott rang up the following Thursday, and said he had been told he could bring Dympna home on the Saturday, and would I get Mrs. Sutton to prepare the bedroom for her.

It was a lovely pink and pale grey bedroom, overlooking the back of the house. It had been her old bedroom before she married, and had been redecorated as a double bedroom for her to share with Gerald when they stayed at Rosenwell. Now I helped Mrs. Sutton to make up the bed and Ena Makin arrived to give the already immaculate room yet another polish. On impulse I went out into the garden and picked a small posy of flowers and leaves, arranging them prettily in a vase I found in the kitchen. The room looked delightful, but I wandered around nervously. Would Dympna be pleased to be home again? Would I be able to cope with her? I was now about to keep my share of the bargain I had made with Elliott.

I don't know what I had expected, but it certainly wasn't the tall, quiet fair-haired woman who walked in with Elliott two days later. I don't know, either, what Elliott had told her about me, but she came forward and took my hand, studying me keenly for a few moments, then she smiled and kissed my cheek.

'I'm very happy that Elliott has married at last,' she said. 'We were beginning to think he would never take the plunge before . . . before it was too late.'

She had noticed my pregnancy and I blushed vividly, so that she laughed again. In one thing Elliott had been correct. Dympna was pleased about the baby.

'I'm glad that . . . that you're pleased and that you're home again, Mrs. Moryson.'

Her smile vanished in an instant and I saw what the 'difficult' side of her nature could look like . . . almost like the fierce glow of a cat who had spotted an enemy.

'Don't call me that,' she said, sharply. 'You're Elliott's wife. You must call me Dympna.'

'Dympna.'

I managed a wan smile, so that her mood changed again.

'Elliott is naughty, not bringing you to meet me long ago when you first became friendly. I believe you went to Malamba Island with him.'

'Yes.'

'It isn't to be wondered at that you fell in love against such a romantic setting, but it seems to have turned out happily for you both.'

I saw Elliott glancing at me, and wished he had clued me in before I met his sister. I was aware of him standing very still, as though waiting for my answer.

'It has turned out very happily,' I agreed.

Mrs. Sutton, coming in with a tray of tea and refreshments just to 'put us on' till we sat down to dinner, beamed. I had no doubt she had heard some of the conversation and it had answered a few of her own questions. Now I could sense that the reserve she had felt towards me had melted.

'Mrs. Elliott has been getting everything shipshape for you coming home, Miss Dympna,' she said. 'She's settled in very nicely, and we're going to sort out the old nursery next week, if Mr. Elliott approves.'

'I leave that to . . . to you women,' said Elliott, uncomfortably, and again I could feel the hot colour in my cheeks.

'I'm sure we can manage without troubling you, Elliott,' I managed, evenly.

'You must let me help,' said Dympna, drinking a cup of hot tea with obvious enjoyment. 'It's something I'd love to do.'

Elliott's eyes met mine, and I thought I saw gratitude and a hint of relief in them. Dympna was going to react exactly as he had predicted, but what happened after she had settled into her old home and my baby was born? What would happen then? Her eventual true happiness would lie in a return to her own home and her husband. Somehow I felt that *that* particular task was going to be as great as one of the Labours of Hercules. And I was supposed to accomplish that!

But first I would really have to get to

know Dympna Moryson, and while we all drank tea and laughed happily round a cosy fire in the lounge of Rosenwell that Saturday afternoon, I felt that I didn't know a thing about her, or even how to avoid the casual word which could change her from a quiet, charming woman to one who was wary-looking and almost violent, ready to hit out at whatever was likely to hurt her.

Elliott stayed with us at Rosenwell for a couple of days before he had to leave for London again. He brought me a tray of tea and biscuits early on that morning, and sat down on the edge of the bed while I struggled up to a sitting position after a deep but troubled sleep.

'You look like a sleepy child,' he said, smiling wryly.

'I feel ninety,' I told him and the smile faded.

'It's going to be difficult, now, for you to back away from our bargain,' he said, rather heavily, 'and the longer I consider it, the more I think I must have been out of my mind to ask you to do it. I'd forgotten that as time went on, you would lose a bit of your physical strength, and perhaps would not be able to cope with Dympna.'

I swallowed. 'You . . . you mean she gets violent?'

'Good Lord no! She's never been that . . . except for that one time she caused the accident. And that was to Gerald. With everyone else she's never been anything but quiet and courteous.'

I nodded and tried to look convinced, though I was shaking inside, and managed to cover it up by drinking some of the hot tea.

'She seems to have taken to you,' Elliott went on. 'I've had a drubbing for not telling her about you before now, and bringing you to meet her. She . . . she's been at me many times to marry . . . '

'But you never met anyone you really cared for?'

His face grew rather hard.

'I felt that marriage was out of the

question for me.'

Suddenly I had one of those flashes of insight which strikes one from time to time. Elliott was afraid there was a taint in the family, having seen how unstable Dympna had become. That was why he didn't want to have his own children. He was afraid. It might suit him very well to share my child, if he could learn to care for it.

Yet that was nonsense. After Dympna was better, and in a reasonable space of time, he would want us to separate. I looked at his handsome dark head, and again I could feel the sadness deep inside. If only things had been different. If only . . . if only it was a normal marriage and Elliott loved me. If only I was having his child . . . how happy things could be for me, at least. I would learn to love Dympna as my true sister, and do my best for her. My own happiness might overflow to her. Gradually I was realizing that I had begun to love my own husband, but the fact that we were married under such circumstances seemed to make things worse instead of better. 'I'll do my best for Dympna,' I told Elliott, quietly.

For him I felt I would go through any agony, whether physical or mental. 'Try not to worry. I'm sure we'll build up a relationship. Just give us time. I'll encourage her to go walking with me . . . only a short distance, and she can show me the local countryside. I haven't met any neighbours yet either. Aren't there any more people to meet?'

Too late I realized he would have no wish to encourage the gossip of neighbours. They were bound to be curious about Dympna . . . and me.

'A retired Royal Naval Commander and his wife, and the Dixons who spend most of their lives abroad and leave Brookfield Grange to a caretaker. I haven't had much time to keep up to date with what is going on in the village, about three miles away.'

'That's all right. I don't really want to know. I was only thinking it might be something for Dympna to do, but we'll find plenty here at home.'

Suddenly he bent and kissed me, though it was a gentle kiss such as he might give to a friend. Yet it would be nice if he thought of me as a friend. Often couples marry because they're in love, but underneath they never learn to be friends. That was one reason why I would never have married Mike.

'I'm glad you're here,' he said, simply, 'though you must promise to get on that telephone as soon as you feel things might become too much for you.'

'I promise.'

'It's funny . . . you look . . .'

He paused as though searching for a word. 'Never mind. I'm glad you can cope.'

Once again he had donned his usual exterior of quiet efficiency, and it seemed as though I had been imagining the cosy feeling of closeness between us. He was the man I thought of as Dr. Manley.

'I'm going now. Goodbye, my dear. I

should be back in a few days.'

'Goodbye, Elliott.'

He picked up the tray and walked quietly to the door, closing it behind him without looking back. I looked at the time and wished I could sleep for another hour, but I was now thoroughly awake. Slipping out of bed, I ran a bath and luxuriated for a little while, then I dressed slowly and walked downstairs to my little room where Mrs. Sutton found me an hour later, exclaiming over the dead fire. I hardly heard her scoldings for sitting in a cold room. My mind was full of thoughts, not all of them unpleasant.

* * *

The weather had been capricious, with cold days in summer and the hint of an Indian summer in autumn. For a few days Dympna and I walked along country lanes wearing only cotton shirts over slacks, my own rather voluminous. Elliott had booked me in at a nursing home a few miles away, and had asked Dympna, quietly, to look after me. This had been a spark of genius on his part, though my position was a strange one. My bargain was that I should look after Dympna, but instead I found myself under her wing practically every hour of the day. She inspected my layette, and insisted on buying wool, knitting laboriously at a matineé coat. She saw to it that I didn't raise my arms above my head, or carried anything very heavy. The doctor called regularly for a 'listen', and I found myself depending on my new sister-in-law more and more.

In odd moments I even realized I was beginning to love her, though one day I made the mistake of answering her idle question as to Elliott's whereabouts with the information that he had gone to see Gerald. Dympna's face went pure white, her eyes almost glaring at me.

'I want to forget about that,' she said, sharply.

'I know. It . . . it must be awful for you . . . very upsetting . . . ' I managed, awkwardly. 'To know that he . . . he's still trying to pull round.'

'I hate him,' said Dympna, venomously. 'There's no use pretending to you. If we're going to be close sisters, I must tell you the truth. I . . . hate . . . him.'

Her eyes blazed at me, and I could feel the cold fingers of fear on my spine, then a wave of sickness enveloped me. We had walked to the village that day, and I knew now that it had been too far.

'What is it? What's the matter?' asked Dympna, her voice normal.

'I . . . I feel queer.'

'I'll telephone the doctor.'

'No! No . . . wait . . . It might pass. Could you get some . . . some tea?'

She got up in a second. Mrs. Sutton was having her evening off and had left us a cold supper, but now Dympna quickly boiled a kettle and brought us a tray of tea. The hardness had gone from her face, and she looked sweet and charming. I knew now that Elliott resembled their mother, while Dympna was a feminine version of their father, who had been fair with classical features. At first sight, one might have overlooked Dympna, thinking her ordinary, but as I came to know her, I could see the fine beauty of her bones, and the soft gold lights in her hair. With proper clothes and make-up, she could be exquisite, but I knew she no longer cared deeply about her own appearance. She did all that was necessary to keep herself neatly clothed and sufficiently well-groomed, but she had no interest in the extra effort it would take to turn her looks into something really special. I wondered if she had ever achieved that, or if she had never realized her own potential.

'You're very pretty,' she said to me one day, as we sat on chairs outside on the terrace, and I allowed the sun to shine warmly on my face.

'But not beautiful, like you,' I said,

smiling, and she turned pink.

'I've never been beautiful.'

I hadn't answered since Mrs. Sutton appeared with a tray of lemonade, but for a day or two Dympna tried one or two new hairstyles, then went back to running a comb through it as usual.

Now it was standing on end a little as she stared at me uncertainly.

'No pains, Berris?'

'No. Just a trifle faint. The tea is very welcome.'

Half an hour later my pains started, and in no time Dympna had telephoned everyone who mattered . . . Elliott . . . the doctor . . . Elliott . . . the nursing home . . . Elliott, again, gradually losing patience when she could not find him at the flat, or the office.

'He was going to Austria,' I said. 'He may have been delayed . . . '

'Lie still,' said Dympna. 'He should be available. At a time like this, with his child arriving . . . he's got no consideration . . . '

'No,' I said, weakly. 'No, don't blame Elliott . . . '

'You're too quick to excuse him. I'll find him for you, Berris dear. Don't you worry.'

I was past worrying. In no time Dympna had the car out and my case deposited in the boot, then she was driving as quickly as she dared for the nursing home.

It was a difficult birth. The umbilical cord was round my baby's neck, and the midwife who had examined me, and said there was plenty of time before summoning the doctor, suddenly was moving very fast indeed, and I was vaguely aware of white-coated figures round the delivery bed while I feebly protested against yet another examination, and was given a nozzle and told to breathe into it.

Time had no meaning for me, and I tried to obey the orders given to me in sharply authoritative tones, though I could only feel a great weight of fatigue.

'Don't push, Mother, don't push,' the

midwife was saying, then I went to sleep as a needle was plunged into the back of my hand.

My dreams were weird and jumbled but it only seemed a moment later when a young nurse was bending over me.

'It's a lovely little girl,' she said.

'A girl,' I repeated. 'A girl.'

I had a daughter. I had a living being in the world who belonged to me. I didn't know I was crying till I felt the wetness of tears trickling into my ears as I listened to my child crying feebly, then much stronger, and I longed to hold her in my arms, though they seemed abnormally heavy. Then I drifted, again, into sleep.

* * *

Elliott flew home from Austria and brought masses of flowers and chocolates. For a while it was easy to forget that we were not a normal couple, drooling over our first baby. Dympna looked years younger as she looked at the baby asleep in a small cot at the end of my bed.

'She's dark, just like Elliott,' she said, and I felt the smile freeze on my face as Elliott's eyes met mine. Then he winked deliberately, and I breathed again.

'She's like herself,' he said to Dympna. 'I think everyone should be born as individuals, and not compared with anyone else.'

'Oh, but it's only natural, surely,' Dympna said, coming to sit by my bedside. 'I mean, to try to trace one's ancestry in one's children. She could look exactly like Mother, lucky girl. Oh, not that she might not favour *your* side too, Berris . . . '

'My father was a redhead,' I said. 'Mother was mouse, but it's so long since I lost them . . . '

'Well, now you've got your own family, and I can't tell you how happy I am for Elliott's sake. You *will* allow me to take an interest in her, won't you, Berris? It's wonderful being an aunt.'

Again Elliott looked at me happily. The experiment seemed to be succeeding beyond his wildest dreams. No one would suspect, looking at the happy, cheerful woman who was now sitting beside us, that she had spent months in a special hospital for the kind of nervous depression from which she had suffered. He took my hand, and I knew it was his way of expressing gratitude.

'Have you thought of a name, Berris?' he asked.

'Oh, she must be Bridget, after Mother,' said Dympna.

'No. She must have her own name,' Elliott insisted, 'or if she must be called after a grandparent, then we'll choose Berris' mother.'

I felt some of my happiness drifting away. Of course Elliott would not want my child to take his mother's name. I had thought of names, on and off, but I preferred the ordinary plain names myself.

'Helen,' I said.

'Not very imaginative,' said Dympna,

'Why not something like Zoe or Deirdre? Or even old-fashioned names like Emily and Hannah? They're coming back again.'

'I like Helen,' said Elliott.

'Helen Dympna,' I said on impulse, and both Elliott and Dympna seemed to stare at me for a moment. I coloured furiously and avoided looking at Elliott. I could have wished the words unsaid. How stupid of me to suggest Dympna's name.

Then she had come to put her arms round my neck and to kiss my cheek, while I saw that Elliott was smiling with gratitude.

'Helen Dympna,' he said. 'What could be nicer?'

'I'll be her godmother,' said Dympna. 'You *will* want me to be godmother?'

'I . . . I . . . '

'Berris is tired. We have heaps of time to discuss godmothers,' said Elliott.

'Well, I'll leave you two together,' said Dympna gaily. 'You never seem to kiss Berris while I'm with you, Elliot. You're so shy. It's a wonder she puts up with you. You're so matter-of-fact you might have been married for years and years.'

She picked up her bag and waved gaily as she left the room. Elliott turned to me, embarrassed, then he bent down and kissed my cheek. I longed to throw my arms round his neck and kiss him properly, but I pretended I was very tired.

'I'll go now,' said Elliott. 'I . . . I'm glad the baby is well.'

'Yes,' I said. 'Yes.'

There seemed little else to say.

'Mrs. Sutton has everything ready for you, at home. Dympna too.'

'Yes,' I said again. 'Thank you for coming, Elliott. I . . . I'm sorry if it is awkward for you.'

He looked grave and rather tired.

'It doesn't have to be. Goodnight, Berris.'

'Goodnight.'

But it was awkward, I thought, as he closed the door . . . how awkward I hadn't visualized until now.

Helen, my baby, had been tiny at birth, weighing barely five and a half pounds, but after her initial loss of weight, she began to grow so that by the time I brought her home to Rosenwell, she had regained her birthweight and was perfectly formed.

Mrs. Sutton went into ecstacies over her, and Rose Makin, was allowed to wheel her out a little each day, in the shiny cream-coloured pram which had been a gift from Dympna. Elliott had wanted to book a nurse to live in for a few weeks, caring for me and the baby, but I vetoed that, feeling that I was already being looked after by enough people, and that he had done enough for me. A visiting nurse called each day to check the baby's weight, and the doctor called to make sure of my own continuing good health, and that no complications had arisen after the birth. But apparently the good Cumbrian air had made a strong young woman of me, able to bear children easily, apart from the one complication during the birth.

Elliott seemed to hover around for a few days, though we rarely had a chance to talk on our own. Always there was Dympna, determined to supervise the baby's welfare till I was strong enough, and Mrs. Sutton who felt obliged to mother all of us, while Rose had been told by Elliott that she would be required to help with the baby, and was equally determined to do her bit. Sometimes I felt like screaming, and sometimes I would answer a question sharply, then go to my room where I would cry without knowing quite why I felt so desolate.

'Post natal depression,' said the nurse, and everyone worked even harder to spoil me, and look after me, so that I longed to shout out the true circumstances and to tell them that I deserved none of it.

This was especially true of Dympna who had begun to love Helen so much that I was growing afraid. I remembered that she was not stable, and though it was hard to imagine any harm coming to my baby through her love, I found myself watching her when she handled Helen, and insisting more and more that Rose should wheel her out, and not Dympna.

'I don't know why Elliott hired the girl, apart from seeing to the baby's clean clothes and things,' Dympna complained. 'He must have known I would do all that was necessary for my own niece.'

'When he hired Rose you were still in . . . in hospital . . . ', I said, then flushed, biting my tongue for reminding her.

'I . . . er . . . I forgot,' she confessed. 'It seems so very far away now, like a different life. It seems as though I've come out of a nightmare.'

It was the first time she had talked of her experiences, and I wondered whether I ought to encourage her to talk, or to forget. It was at times like these that I felt my immaturity, and inadequacy of the task Elliott had set for me.

'Would it help, now, for you to go and see your husband?' I asked her, carefully. 'He's gradually improving in health and might be coming home soon, so that you could begin to think about your future . . . '

She didn't come out with her usual outburst when Gerald's name was mentioned, but I saw that she had grown very pale again.

'How lucky you are, Berris,' she said, after a long silence. 'You don't know, my dear, what it feels like to be as lucky as you, with Elliott for a husband and a beautiful baby like Helen. You just don't know.'

For a long moment I felt like setting her straight. Elliott had been coming to stay less and less in recent weeks, and the less I saw of him, the more I realised I was coming to love him. Sometimes I felt physically sick with my own thoughts. The birth of my child had aroused something in me . . . some sort of basic instinct to do with being a woman, so that I wanted a normal relationship with a normal husband.

What could Dympna know of such a thing? She had a husband who had been gentle with her, by all accounts, and who was handsome above the ordinary, yet somewhere along their marriage she had lost her love for him. She had loved him passionately when they married. I had come across their wedding photographs one day, and one especially caught my eye, of a smiling Gerald staring at the camera, while Dympna had turned to look at him. Her love for him was there for all to see. And Mrs. Sutton had said how much she had admired him.

'Miss Dympna won't talk about it, but I think she had a 'miss',' she said one day. 'She got rushed off to hospital, anyway, and the next time I saw her, she was like a wee ghost. Yet she'd been bonny up till then. Nobody said what was wrong, just that she'd had a 'turn', but it was easy to guess. I think it broke her heart, and she expected Mr. Gerald to feel the same way, but men don't look on things the same as women. Mr. Gerald has his work. He gets absorbed in that. Miss Dympna wanted true family life, and she has too little to do.'

I thought about that many times, and now as I looked at Dympna, with her face full of suffering, and the love growing in her for my own child, I hardly knew how I felt. Was I succeeding in getting her well again, and so helping Elliott, or were new problems being created? Was I any nearer to bringing her to terms with her own future? At least she was no longer like a wild animal when Gerald was mentioned. She grew calm now, but it was the cold calm attitude which reminded me of marble. Sometime I would try to get her to talk about it, but I was still afraid of this quiet attitude. It was no more natural than the wildness I had already seen.

Gradually Rosenwell settled down for the winter, the only disappointment for me being Elliott's frequent absences. Dympna even remarked on it once or twice, but I told her, with confidence, that his work took him abroad a great deal, reminding her that we had met when I went to work for him.

'How rotten for you, Berris,' she said, with sympathy. 'It's so unfair. If your situation had been more like . . . like . . . well, never mind . . . they say that absence makes the heart grow fonder and all that. You can look forward to each reunion.'

'Yes,' I said, and she saw that I didn't want to discuss it.

There were few changes, but from Dympna's point of view, the happiest one came when Rose Makin was accepted for training as a nurse, and came to say that she hoped to leave soon. I was happy for the girl, and Ena Makin was obviously pleased that I encouraged her daughter.

Happiest of all was Dympna. She decided that no one else need be hired to help out with Helen. She could do all that was necessary, besides myself. I was not entirely happy with the state of affairs, though Dympna never set out to take my baby from me. She always gave me my place as Helen's mother, but her whole day seemed to be wrapped up in helping to do the hundred and one jobs which crop up, while looking after a child.

The old house grew cosy in winter. The cost of oil for central heating had gone sky-high, but Elliott did not seem to mind the bills. There were plenty of small trees which had fallen in the woods during a freak storm the previous winter, and John Makin sawed them up, so that we had huge log fires, even in my small room. I began to accept this way of life, and to enjoy it. Being brought up at Highfield, I could adjust easily to country living . . . something which Elliott had taken into consideration, I was quite sure, when he made me his proposition.

Dympna was also gradually looking younger and younger. I think we both bloomed that winter. We had Helen to look after and Mrs. Sutton to cook for us. A few local ladies called, and we formed one or two friendships, though the inaccessibility of Rosenwell from the village was a help in that direction since neither Dympna nor I wanted to be too close to any outsider.

The cost of petrol was prohibitive, and also the walk in the cold winter days. We supported coffee mornings given to raise money for Charities, and found a variety of things for White Elephant Stalls. I even baked scones and cakes from all the old recipes I had learned at home for the Cake Stalls and was greatly complimented. I found that my position as Elliott's wife earned me a great deal of respect, and I learned that no one so far, had found out the real truth behind my relationship with Elliott. It had been assumed that we lived in London, or abroad, and even in Cumbria before I came to Rosenwell, no doubt because the Manley children were all born there.

Elliott came home again before Christmas, and asked me if I would like a trip to town to buy some gifts. I could sense that this was just a cover for him to discuss things with me, but Dympna leapt at the idea.

'Yes, you go Berris,' she insisted, 'though it's too cold to take Helen. She's used to a warm house. Leave her with me, dear. You know I'll look after her as though . . . as though she were my own.'

I hesitated. I had grown to love my baby passionately, so that even a few days away from her would make me feel deprived. She was still too young to miss me too much, though I knew she would. But Dympna had handled her almost as much as I had, and the baby would not suffer by my absence.

'Come on, my love,' said Elliott. 'You can leave your baby for two days, surely.'

It was a slip of the tongue and Dympna frowned.

'Your baby, too,' she said, sharply.

'Honestly . . . you men! I'm beginning to think you're all alike.'

I could see the nervous twitch at her left eye again, but as Elliott grinned at her, she suddenly leaned over and gave him one of her rare kisses.

'Sorry, my dear brother, I'm a cross-patch. But Berris is such a wonderful mother to this daughter of yours. I'll do my best for her, Berris dear . . . really I will.'

'All right,' I agreed, then glanced uncertainly at Elliott. 'Shall I pack a weekend bag?'

'Certainly. We'll stay at the flat. We can leave in the morning.'

We were still occupying separate bedrooms but Elliott got round that by remarking that he had been sleeping badly recently.

'Too many Atlantic crossings,' he said. 'The time factor is a hazard for me.'

'I hope you can have a good rest over Christmas,' said Dympna. 'You need a week or two at home, here, where it is quiet. It's the finest palliative I know.'

She was looking so well, with faint apricot colour in her cheeks, so that I could see how lovely she had been . . . indeed, how lovely she was now. She seemed a plain girl at first, beside her husband, but now I saw that she was truly beautiful.

5

We left for London early the following morning. I wore a new misty-blue suit which Dympna had helped me to choose one day when we went shopping, and found a small, but delightful, boutique. I knew I had matured since Helen was born, and felt that I was looking my best. Elliott had given me an approving look, but though we had been at ease with one another at Rosenwell, suddenly I felt shy of him, and we drove in silence for some time, then stopped by a small wayside tearoom for a cup of coffee.

As we waited for it to be brought, I glanced round the tearoom which was bright and pleasant, but empty of patrons except for ourselves, then looked at Elliott. He was gazing at me.

'We haven't talked much recently, have we, Berris?'

My heart leapt. Did he feel, now, that my part in his life was over? Did he feel that Dympna was now well enough to get on without me? I grew cold and shivery at the thought.

'No.'

'How . . . how do you find Dympna?' he asked, stirring sugar into his coffee.

'She seems happy now,' I said, 'though . . . '

'Though?'

'I can't speak for how she will react when . . . when she goes back to her husband. I don't think she's been happy with him.'

Elliott drew a hand through his hair.

'It doesn't make sense,' he said. 'I saw how much they loved one another, right from the start. Then she just seemed to change, though Gerald has done everything to make her happy . . . everything. No man could have done more. Yet, she treats him as though he were an . . . an animal or something, whose feelings can be trampled upon, and insulted.'

'No . . . surely not.'

'I've seen them together. You haven't. Besides, you've got to know Dympna, but you don't really know Gerald. That's why I want you to meet him again, Berris.'

I bit my lip.

'You think that will help?'

'I can't think of anything else to do. You see, Gerald is due to be discharged, soon, from hospital. He has nowhere to go, except to us. Their home is shut up for the moment, and he can't go to that cold house unless there is a staff to look after him. So you see my problem? Somehow we must find what has turned my sister against her husband. Somehow they must resolve their differences.'

I nodded. 'If she is no longer in love with him, then couldn't they just separate?'

'Is Dympna well enough to go and live somewhere on her own? Is Gerald? They're both recovering from a bad accident. I have to take them into my home. They have nowhere else to go.'

'I suppose so.'

'Your home, too,' he amended, hastily, but I shook my head.

'Not really. You know that our marriage is . . . ' I almost said it was in a worse state than Dympna's, but thought they could hardly be compared, except that it was I who loved Elliott, while he cared little for me. Yet I felt he liked me, and certainly did not bear me animosity, as Dympna did for Gerald.

'I thought we would go and see Gerald before going to the flat.'

'Was that the real reason you wanted me to come to London with you?' I asked, unreasonably disappointed.

In spite of myself, I had been building a few dreams round the visit.

'Not at all. It's time you had a little fun,' said Elliott heartily.

But I didn't believe him.

Gerald Moryson looked much stronger and fitter than he had been the last time I had seen him. He greeted me warmly and immediately asked after his wife. I told him, rather carefully, that she was well and seemed to be filling her days very happily by looking after baby Helen. For a moment I caught the flicker of something in his eyes again, then he began to talk eagerly about Dympna, and how pleased he was that she was regaining her health.

'It's all been for the best,' he said to Elliott. 'That I do believe. Dympna was gradually losing her stamina, and it made her a bit . . . well . . . cross, so that she seemed to be going downhill all the time. I think the crunch came when we had our accident, and now she's building up again and it's just wonderful. It's worth all these weeks in hospital, just to have our old life back again.'

His eyes glowed and I could see now how Elliott must feel about his brother-in-law. There was a sort of naïvety about him, a sort of implicit trust that everything would come right in the end. But underneath I felt a deep unease. Dympna wasn't really well enough yet to go back to the beginning. Her new good health and spirits was only a veneer. Deep down there was still this peculiar revulsion of feeling she had for Gerald. Her love had turned to hate, or she thought it had. Something he had done, or said, had altered her whole attitude towards him, though it looked as though he, himself, had no idea what it could be.

'I'm so looking forward to being back at Rosenwell,' he told Elliott. 'It has always seemed to be my home, ever since I used to come home with you in the old days. Then, when I married Dympna, I felt I really belonged there. Oh . . . Berris, my dear, I ought not to be talking like this. I forget that you are now the mistress of Rosenwell.'

'I've made no changes to the place,' I said, quickly, glancing at Elliott.

Gerald's eyes were on both of us, obviously curious, and no doubt thinking I was either very accommodating, or very colourless. Few wives made no changes at all to an inherited home. I had not even altered the cover of a cushion!

'How long before you can come home, Gerald?' Elliott asked.

'Another week, I believe, if the results of tests to be taken are satisfactory. I shall get about, you know, but only with a small wheelchair where possible, and a couple of sticks for the awkward places.'

'I'd better try to find you a male nurse, and we can set aside a couple of rooms . . . '

'Nonsense, Elliott. Male nurses are not easy to find and besides, I couldn't put you to the expense, and my own funds will scarcely cover such attention. My investments are sound enough, but the returns are eaten away by inflation, if we must talk business. No, I shall manage perfectly, and Dympna will no doubt be more than happy to help me, as she once did, when she gets used to the idea. She was so competent at looking after me, was my Dympna.'

He was so sure that everything would be all right between them. Shouldn't he be forewarned, I wondered, rather desperately?

'Wouldn't you like her to come and see you before . . . before you come home?' I asked.

'Good Lord no! That's the last thing I'd like. She hates hospitals. That's one reason she won't have anything to do with me in here. She'll only start to be happy again when the memory of hospital life for both of us starts to fade.'

That could be a point, I acknowledged to myself, cheering up a little. The human mind and emotions are so complex, as I very well knew looking at Elliott, that Dympna might well have persuaded herself that she hated Gerald, when she really hated the thought of him lying here in hospital.

'Berris will arrange for you to be comfortable when you come home, I'm quite sure,' said Elliott, smiling at me.

'Of course I will, Mr. Moryson.'

‘Oh *Gerald* . . . surely . . . ’

‘Sorry . . . Gerald,’ I managed, though I found it difficult to think of him with any degree of intimacy. Elliott had said that he had a wonderful brain, and spent hours at his books and his desk. I could understand that. Perhaps that was the secret of his beauty, that the stresses and strains of life passed him by, immersed as he was in scholarly pursuits.

‘We must go now,’ Elliott was saying, and I stood up with more alacrity than was polite.

‘Of course. Goodbye, Gerald; till next week.’

He took my hand. ‘Goodbye, my dear. Thank you for looking after my wife.’

The words were gently said, but the tone was so poignant that I wanted to cry. He really did love Dympna. Somehow I must find a way of bringing them together again.

After we had left the nursing home, Elliott was again very silent, as we drove towards London, and I knew his thoughts were still with his friend.

'Elliott . . . couldn't a Marriage Guidance Counsellor help Dympna?' I asked, and he made no reply for a moment so that I thought he hadn't heard.

'I have already suggested that to Gerald,' he said, after a while, 'but he says he would feel too humiliated to take his marriage problems to anyone else, however skilled. I . . . I didn't even put it to Dympna. A Counsellor can only help if both parties are willing to discuss their problems. Anyway, I can't see Dympna being any more cooperative. Can you?'

I shook my head. No, Dympna was never too eager to go into any details over Gerald. I thought about the coming weeks and swallowed again, nervously. I was not looking forward to being under the same roof as Dympna *and* Gerald. I felt all my new maturity melting away, as I viewed the future with apprehension. Suddenly Elliott's hand was covering mine.

'Don't worry too much,' he said, gently, 'I'll see that they get plenty of skilled help . . . a nurse for Gerald, and perhaps someone extra for you and Dympna.'

'I doubt if that will be necessary,' I said, quickly. I couldn't imagine Dympna welcoming a nurse. Then a thought struck me.

'How . . . I mean, what made you think I was worrying?'

'You catch your breath,' he said. 'I always notice.'

Somehow I found this oddly endearing and comforting, that he should notice any idiosyncracies which I had. Then we were both quiet as he began to negotiate the London traffic before reaching the flat.

Elliott gave me the key.

'Open the door for us, there's a good girl,' he said. 'I'll bring up the cases, and garage the car. We could have a quick wash and change, then pop round to a nice little Greek restaurant I know for a meal. Does that appeal?'

Suddenly I was wildly happy, determined to put the worries of Dympna and Gerald behind me for a couple of days, while we were in London. I was reminding myself that I was Elliott's wife, and for the first time I felt we were truly married.

I luxuriated in a scented bath, not troubling to wonder where the pretty bath salts had come from, and changed into a dark green velvet skirt with a creamy lace top. I had a soft woollen shawl to drape round my shoulders.

Elliott, too, looked elegant in a plain dark suit and white shirt, and I must have looked happy as we went down in the lift, because he put an arm round my shoulders, and kissed me lightly.

'This is lovely,' I said. 'Suddenly I've got an appetite.'

'It's a pleasure to go out with someone . . . with you, Berris, since you *do* take such pleasure in everything. I get a bit jaded at times.'

'Well, tonight everything is going to

be wonderful. We'll just forget all our worries, and leave them at home in Rosenwell.'

'Then you think of it as home?' he asked.

I drew back a little. It wouldn't always be my home.

'For now,' I said, lightly. 'But of course.'

'Of course,' he agreed, ' . . . for now.'

We ate a delicious consommé, then I ordered a chicken curry which brought tears to my eyes and made my nose pink. Elliott found my weepy state highly amusing, but promised me some delicious ice cream if I managed to dispose of all the curry. His own steak had caused no problems, and he laughed a lot while I worked my way through each mouthful. I was to remember the evening for a long time, and to cling to the happiness it gave me.

We lingered a long time over coffee, and Elliott asked me a lot about my childhood, and about my mother and father, especially Father's paintings and how he had worked on them.

'He would have been so proud that they are now sought after,' I said. 'He used to feel frustrated that the critics could not see their merit. I think that was why he . . . ', I paused, biting my lip, then finished quietly, ' . . . why he drank rather a lot.'

'It must have been hard for your mother, Berris.'

I nodded, again touched by his perception.

'Yes. It hurt her that he needed to lose himself in . . . in alcohol. She already gave him so much.'

'Especially a charming daughter.'

I blushed. 'Not so charming. I . . . I let them down, even though I did it after they were both dead.'

'We are all weak creatures, my dear,' said Elliott, and I had never loved him more.

Going back to the flat, I again felt shy of Elliott. The last time we had been alone together had been before Helen was born, and now I felt that things were different. Now I wondered if Elliott would wish to share my room.

I made coffee for us both, and carried it into the lounge where Elliott was watching the late night news, and somehow I felt that he, too, was ill-at-ease. I saw him glancing at me uncertainly from time to time. Finally I rose and carried our tray back to the kitchen, washing up the crockery and leaving everything tidy. My heart was beating faster than usual and when I returned to the kitchen, Elliott was standing by the window with the curtains drawn back.

The small light above the television was the only light in the room, and I came to stand beside him, so that he put his arm round my shoulders and drew me close. I felt a wave of sheer happiness sweep over me as we looked out on a scene of London which I loved every bit as Highfield, or . . . now . . . Rosenwell. They were all very dear to me.

'Will you want us to be properly married, Elliott?' I asked quietly.

His hand tightened on my shoulder and I turned so that he drew me into his arms.

'Have you any protection?' he asked.

'Protection?'

'You know what I mean.' His voice was suddenly rough.

'No.'

'Neither have I. I don't think it would be wise, my dear. You . . . you wouldn't want another child yet.'

I wanted to tell him that I would bear his child with great happiness and pride, but instead I felt oddly hurt, as well as frustrated. I was a normal young woman, but Elliott could not have learned to care very much for me when he viewed our relationship so clinically.

'I . . . I see.'

'No, you don't see,' he said, turning away. 'I . . . I don't want children. I don't want a child who . . . who may grow up like Dympna. I wouldn't like my child to inherit the unstable streak which is obviously in my family.'

'But that's nonsense,' I said. 'Your sister isn't a mad woman.'

'Isn't she? Then how do you account for her behaviour? She has everything to make her happy, but now look at her. How would I feel, or you as my wife feel, if we had children who grew up as unstable, and know that we could have prevented their unhappiness . . . that they need not have been born.'

'Then . . . it isn't just me?'

Elliott didn't reply, but I could feel the strain in him.

'Go to bed, Berris,' he said curtly. 'We'll talk in the morning. I'll have to go to the office, but you can shop for anything you need during the day. I'm hoping to book for a theatre in the evening. It will be a break for you.'

'Don't bother if your only concern is to entertain me,' I told him. 'It isn't necessary.'

'I intend to book for *both* of us,' he said, calmly. 'Go to bed, my dear.'

I bit my lip, but managed to keep a

sense of dignity.

'Goodnight, Elliott.'

'Goodnight.'

Next day Elliott brought me tea in bed again, before leaving for the office, and the daily cleaning woman had arrived by the time I got out of bed. The day was bright with sunshine, the sort of crisp invigorating day which makes winter delightful, and when I had eaten breakfast, I dressed carefully, and took the Underground to the city centre, delighting in the shops once more.

I was determined not to think too much about my relationship with Elliott, and with the resilience of youth, I found I was enjoying my day. I bought a few necessary items of clothing, then visited a large shop which specialized in baby clothing, delighting in the pretty dresses and jackets available for baby girls. Mostly I chose something practical, except for one frothy pink and white dress which I knew would delight Dympna as much as it did myself.

I bought a lovely silk scarf which I knew would match one of Dympna's favourite suits, as well as one or two small gifts for Mrs. Sutton and the Makins. I even bought some linen handkerchiefs for Gerald, then I looked at a new novel by a favourite author of Elliott's, and wondered if he had already bought the book, then took a chance on it.

I had lunch in a charming restaurant, then took a taxi back to the flat, more than satisfied with my day. Elliott was taking me to the theatre that evening, and in spite of the fact that our marriage was a sham, I had begun to *feel* as though I were Elliott's wife, and to act accordingly. I felt very different from the untried girl who had first gone to work for him.

I was humming a tune as I unpacked my purchases, when the bell shrilled loudly. I laid aside a soft toy and went to open the door. Stella Sutton and I stared at one another.

'Elliott, my dear, I . . . ' she began,

then almost immediately she was gasping, 'What are *you* doing here?'

I blinked. Had Elliott been in touch with his secretary again? If so, why hadn't he told her he had married?

'Please come in, Mrs. Sutton,' I invited, thinking how different she looked from the other Mrs. Sutton at Rosenwell. They couldn't have been more a contrast.

She stood still, staring at me for a long moment, then marched into the flat, her gaze going to the packages I had just opened, and the wrapping paper etc. which I was folding up tidily. Her expression cleared.

'Oh, been sent out shopping, have you? I heard you had left, though. I didn't know you were back in the office.'

I bit my lip, wishing Elliott had been here to set things straight, then I decided that she had to know some time. And, anyway, why should it concern Stella Sutton? She was only an ex-employee of the firm, after all.

'I live here, Mrs. Sutton,' I said evenly. 'Dr. Manley and I are married . . . '

She went chalk-white, then sat down suddenly on the nearest chair.

'I don't believe you!'

'I'm sorry you didn't know but it's true nevertheless. I've been living at Rosenwell, but I came up to town to do some shopping.'

She was staring at the soft toys.

'Are those for . . . for *your* child?'

I swallowed and nodded. If she probed further, I would have to put an end to the conversation. I had no intention of discussing my private affairs with Stella Sutton.

Suddenly she was on her feet.

'I can't stay here to talk to you. I'll talk to Elliott another time.'

She hurried towards the door, then turned to stare at me again.

'Nothing of this makes sense. That Elliott should marry *you* . . . '

My inner joy and contentment drained away after she left. Somehow she had managed to rob me of the peace and tranquility which I had gradually been acquiring, and which was giving me confidence in myself. Stella Sutton had not acted like a normal ex-employee of the firm, but more as though she and Elliott had known one another very well indeed.

That evening I had already bathed and changed when Elliott came home. He looked tired and rather preoccupied, but he smiled when he saw me wearing my new creamy-white silk dress which showed that I was in very good health after the fresh air and good food at Rosenwell. I ought to have looked pale and strained after Stella Sutton's visit, but somehow I didn't. It had been cancelled out by the excitement of getting dressed up again, and going out on the sort of date with Elliott which would have been beyond my wildest dreams at one time.

In an odd sort of way Stella had brought this home to me, and I could not help relishing the thought of my new position, even though my house was probably built on sand.

'Hello, my dear . . . all set?' asked Elliott. 'You look very lovely,' he said, gently, and I felt that he meant it.

'Pour me a drink, there's a good girl, and I'll just have a bath and change. Sorry I'm late, but you know how things come up.'

'None better,' I said, and his eyes sobered as though he didn't want to be reminded that he had married his typist from the office.

'Yes . . . well . . . I'll be as quick as I can.'

I loved him, but I was not close to him, I thought, as I waited, leafing over a magazine in front of the lounge fire. If I'd been a proper wife, I would have been eagerly showing him my purchases, and getting ready in between times while we both laughed a lot, and gossiped. But the gulf between us was even wider than it had been when I was in the office. There we had worked together in harmony and contentment.

Now I had a different job to do which was half and between.

I sighed, feeling immature and uncertain again, but pulled myself together as Elliott appeared, immaculately dressed, his well-cut hair so neatly shaped to his head.

'A small whiskey and water?' I asked. 'Right?'

'Right.'

He suddenly grinned at me, and I relaxed.

'This is nice, Berris. I like coming home to the flat when it isn't cold and empty. I can see I'll have to take you back home to Rosenwell soon, or I might be keeping you here to myself.'

I felt my cheeks colour. That was an attractive thought! I had been going to tell him about Stella's visit, but now I said nothing as he picked up my wrap.

'Time to go, my dear. You'd better wear this. It's warmer in here than outside.'

* * *

It was a comedy, but one which probably depended a great deal on the mood of the audience. That evening we were lucky, and joined in the laughter which was infectious. We had dined well, and were in the mood to be entertained. I forgot my worries, and so did Elliott. The problems of Dympna and Gerald seemed very far away and even my baby did not fill my whole mind and a great deal of my heart. I knew she would be having excellent care, and though my arms felt curiously empty, I seemed to revert a little to what I had been before she was conceived, a young girl having a happy time on an evening out. Except that this was a more luxurious evening out than I had ever known in those days, and Elliott a much more elegant and sophisticated escort than anyone else I had known.

Perhaps things might have been different between us if I had forgotten all about Stella Sutton, after we arrived back home to the flat, and Elliott poured us both a nightcap, as we sat down to talk over the play, and to laugh at a favourite piece of dialogue. Some of my purchases were still shrewn about since Stella had interrupted me while I was putting them tidily into a box. Looking round I was suddenly reminded of her visit, and had told Elliott without stopping to consider that it might be a jarring note for him.

'Stella Sutton . . . Mrs. Sutton . . . called to see you this afternoon.'

The laughter went from his eyes.

'Oh yes? Did she leave a message?'

'Only that she would see you again. Elliott . . . she didn't know . . . about me.'

'Why should she?' he asked, coldly. 'Why should I discuss my private affairs with an ex-employee?'

The word hung between us. I was an ex-employee. In fact, if you got down to basics, I might not even be 'ex'. Elliott picked up his glass and tossed back his drink.

'I'll drive you home to Rosenwell in

the morning,' he said. 'I'll be informing Dympna that Gerald is due to come home soon. I look on you to put her in a happy frame of mind for his return.'

'I . . . I don't think she loves him enough now,' I said. 'I think that's where the fault lies.'

'How many people try to destroy the lives of their partners just because their initial passion wears off? Where would the world be if we all did that?'

I said nothing more, but gathered up my wrap and went towards my bedroom.

'Goodnight, Elliott,' I said.

'Goodnight, Berris. Try to get a good sleep, before the journey to Rosenwell.'

I nodded and closed the door. The laughter had gone. I was back to reality once again. Now I must get to work on Dympna, and try to make her face her future life with Gerald. She, who did not want her husband, was going to be made to accept him. I, who did, would then lose mine.

6

We travelled back to Rosenwell the following morning, both of us rather silent, though I forgot to be depressed as we neared the lovely old house which I was coming to love rather too much. I suppose Elliott must have seen the delight on my face as we came within sight of the pillars and the drive up to the front of the house.

'Are you glad to be home?' he asked, 'or is it the thought of seeing the baby which is making you come to life again?'

'A bit of both, I guess,' I said, honestly. 'I have missed Helen, and I've missed Rosenwell, too. It will be sad when . . . when I have to leave it all some time.'

He said nothing and I saw that he was frowning, so that I felt a fool. Why does one speak heedlessly at times, then blush all over with shame? It's a failing I have never been able to control. I didn't want Elliott to think I had already started a campaign against being thrown out when Dympna went home to her husband.

But I couldn't stay chastened for long, as Dympna and Mrs. Sutton appeared from nowhere to greet us. The baby was sleeping, having already been bathed and put to bed, but I lost no time in running up to the bright nursery, and looking at my tiny daughter. She seemed to have filled out even in a few days, and as I leaned over the cot, I found that Elliott was standing beside me.

'She looks well,' he commented. 'She's a pretty child.'

I felt pleased and rather touched by his gesture until I realised that it would look odd if he didn't come and see the baby.

I unpacked the gifts I had brought, sharing in Dympna's delight, until Elliott reminded us that he had to leave again after a meal. He was in a mood during the meal, but Dympna asked eagerly about the theatre, and if I had seen anything nice in the way of fashion. Towards the end of the meal, Elliott suddenly came to life and informed Dympna that we had been to see Gerald. She went pale, her face suddenly pinched and old, though she said nothing, but looked down at her plate. Elliott viewed her with exasperation.

'Berris will tell you about it,' he said. 'I have no time to go into details.'

He looked at me beseechingly, and I nodded. It was part of my job, I realised, to start softening up Dympna, though another look at her face made me curl inwardly. It was not going to be all that easy.

Yet Dympna took the news of Gerald's return home very quietly when I told her all about it later that evening. I had decided to leave it until the following day as she was obviously in a mood, but at bed-time I found I could not sleep until I'd had a talk with her, and padded along to her bedroom in my dressing gown. I knew she didn't go to sleep early, but often read travel books into the early hours of the morning.

When I knocked lightly, there was silence for a moment, and I thought Dympna had either gone to sleep after all, or did not want to talk to me, but after a moment she called for me to come in.

She was sitting up in bed, and it seemed as though she had just been staring into space as her book was closed and her spectacles lay on top of it.

'I thought I'd better come and tell you about . . . about Gerald. You must be wondering.' She stared at me almost sightlessly, and I felt chilled by what I saw on her face.

'Why do you hate him so much?' I asked, suddenly feeling I must try to get to the bottom of what was troubling her. 'Elliott said you were so much in love . . . at first.'

'Elliott was right.'

Her voice was almost jagged, and I could see that she was holding herself under control, but with strain. If only I could make her cry, it might help.

'He seems to care so much for you in . . . in spite of everything,' I said. 'Don't you know that, Dympna?'

'Yes, I know that.'

'Then . . . can't you talk about it?'

She was eyeing me thoughtfully, as though trying to make up her mind.

'You wouldn't understand.'

'Try me.'

'No. You're too young. I know you're Elliott's wife, and my sister-in-law, but I'm several years older . . . almost old enough to be your mother, or a much older sister. Your quiet life among the Cumbrian mountains hasn't fitted you for understanding people like Gerald.'

Sudden inspiration flooded through me.

'He's homosexual,' I said.

Her mouth opened with shock, then

she went scarlet.

'He's no such thing. How could you even suggest such a thing!'

We *were* of a different generation. Dympna was of an age when it was difficult to discuss anything of this kind. Yet I knew by her reaction that I was away off the mark.

'Then he bothered you too much?'

She was even more offended. 'My dear Berris, I know you mean well, but you're wasting your time. There was nothing wrong with our . . . our intimate relationship. I've told you I can't discuss my marriage with you . . . or with Elliott, come to that. He would only see Gerald's point of view.'

'Marriage Guidance?'

'What good could anything like that do? You don't understand. There's . . . there's no protection against someone like Gerald.'

'Wouldn't he talk to a counsellor?'

'Oh yes, he'd talk. He'd do anything, I'm sure. He'd accept their advice and be full of sweet reason. *I'd* be the one who . . . who would curl up inside. I can't talk to anyone, and I wish you'd try to influence Elliott into making other provisions for Gerald, and not bring him here. It doesn't help. He thinks we've only got to see one another again, and I'll be in Gerald's arms. Nothing could be further from the truth.'

I bit my lip. 'He seems to be . . . fond of Gerald. I think he wants to do what is best for him as well as you.'

'But this is my old home, Berris. I find it hard to express my feelings now, but I'm very grateful that you haven't made me feel it is *your* home, and I'm not welcome here. It's been like the old days, only better, because Elliott's wife is here, and his child . . . '

'Not . . . ' I began, then bit back the words. Would it make things worse if I made a clean breast of everything to Dympna? I felt as though I were treading on eggs.

'When is he coming?' she asked, tonelessly, after a while.

'Next Sunday.'

I watched her sitting so still as though there was a frightened bird beating inside her, longing to escape and fly away. I thought about Gerald and his confidence that Dympna would be here to welcome him back home again, having got over her temporary bout of 'nerves', which often leads an unstable person to turn against the one closest to them. I could see now that Elliott was right about Dympna. She *was* unstable. I could see, too, the tragedy in his life when he felt he could not have children in case this would come out in a new generation. If he had cared about me more, he might have wanted to accept Helen as his own child, knowing she was his in the eyes of the world, yet without the taint of Manley blood. Watching Dympna, my heart ached for Elliott, as well as for her.

'Oh Dympna,' I whispered, 'if only there was something I could do.'

She smiled at me gently.

'It's not your worry or concern, my dear. Go back to bed. Only . . . we've got to discuss Helen, and her future, in the morning. She's more important than either of us. Gerald must not be allowed to see Helen.'

I stood up, my mouth dry. She looked so normal, yet the words made no sense. Why shouldn't Gerald Moryson see my daughter? What harm could he do her? It was more evidence of Dympna's confused mind.

'We'll talk about it tomorrow,' I placated her. 'Thank you for looking after my baby so well while I was away.'

Privately I was resolving never to leave her alone with Helen again. Who knows what she would be liable to do?

'I loved it,' she said, simply. 'She's a lovely child. She must always come first, Berris.'

I could not quarrel with that.

Dympna was very quiet over the next few days, and took no part in helping Mrs. Sutton and me to prepare a room for Gerald. Elliott was arranging for a private nurse to come and stay to look after his needs, and Mrs. Sutton muttered dark thoughts about these plans, especially when he finally decided on a woman.

'Always wanting you to drop everything and attend to the things they want,' she said, grimly. 'I've known some of them madams in the past.'

'Oh come on, Mrs. Sutton,' I laughed. 'You know they aren't all like that. I've known some very nice girls who do private nursing . . . the nicest, in fact.'

She was so jealous of her position in the household, I realised, and perhaps that was the main reason she had accepted me. I never interfered with the way she ran the house, feeling as I did that it would be a waste of time disrupting anything, since my own stay at Rosenwell was limited.

Dympna had offered to look after Helen while Mrs. Sutton rearranged some of the rooms, though I found myself constantly watching her, ill at ease over the possessive way she held my baby. Helen was good as gold with her, and I could have no complaints over the way Dympna handled her.

One afternoon we spent in the garden, having tea, while Helen slept in the pram, and I found it so much warmer than my native Cumbria that I enjoyed the fresh air very much. This, combined with good food, well cooked, was doing quite a lot for my appearance, not to mention Dympna's guidance with my clothes. I had thought my own taste for plain quiet clothes good enough, but she brought a new eye to styles which suited me, finding unusual trimmings, raising and lowering waist lines, so that I was becoming quite elegant. Christmas had come and gone, and we had spent it very quietly, but I had some pretty new accessories to show for it. In spite of the long tunnel which lay ahead, I was happy.

'This is lovely,' I said. 'It will be growing cold at Highfield again.

Doesn't time fly?'

It was almost a year now since I had taken myself home in disgrace. What a strange year it had been!

'Tell me about Highfield,' Dympna asked.

'Oh . . . nothing much to tell. It's only a cottage. I hear regularly from Mrs. Shorrock who looks after it for me. I love it, though.'

'How do you get there?'

'The M1 Scotch Corner mainly, then the A66 through Appleby.'

'Show me on a map,' she invited, leaping up to go and find an AA book.'

'What's the idea?' I asked her, suspiciously. 'Why do you want to know?'

'You're my sister-in-law, for heaven's sake,' she said, almost crossly. 'I want to know your background. Is that so unusual?'

I felt oddly offended that she wanted to probe into my backgound.

'I know it isn't salubrious,' I told her, 'and I haven't got a very impressive family tree, though my father's paintings are quite well-known now. My mother was the daughter of a hill farmer . . . '

'Oh stop it,' she said. 'You know that isn't what I meant. It's just that your cottage in Cumbria gives me an impression of . . . of romance, for want of a better word. It stirs the imagination. It takes me out of this harsh twentieth century living, and puts me gently down into a past era, if you see what I mean. That's something I find exciting.'

I looked round at Dympna's 'harsh twentieth century living' and thought about Highfield, almost laughing at the absurdity of Dympna's ideas. Instead I found myself tracing a route on the map, showing her where Highfield lay.

'It's like Hugh Walpole, isn't it?' she asked, her eyes shining. 'Oh, how I used to love reading those books. You *will* take me to your cottage some time, won't you, Berris? I'd love to go.'

'Of course I will, if you would really

like to see it. Mrs. Shorrock keeps it well aired, and all in good order. Elliott has made a business arrangement with her, though she does it with love, anyway. She and my aunt, who left it to me, were best friends.'

'Does she live nearby?'

'Yes. It's quite handy for her.'

'It all sounds very attractive,' said Dympna, wistfully.

* * *

Stella Sutton rang up next day, and it was only when Mrs. Sutton came to find me that I began to wonder if they had any connection with one another.

'It's Stella,' she said. 'Mrs. Sutton . . . Paul's wife. She said she'd like to speak with you.'

'Paul's wife?' I repeated, rather stupidly.

'My nephew. He's a clever young man with a fine job in London. We rarely see one another, though I was at his wedding when he married Mr.

Elliott's secretary.'

'Oh . . . Oh yes, of course.'

This news had my head reeling a bit. Somehow I had never connected Mrs. Sutton with Stella! It was obvious they had little contact with one another when Stella had not known about my marriage to Elliott.

'She's a madam,' said Mrs. Sutton, darkly, using her favourite term for women who crossed her. 'Trying to come the lady over me at times. I keep *her* in her place, though. She only married Paul when she saw Mr. Elliott could not be brought up to scratch. He had time to come and see me in those days, and she was always hanging around Rosenwell . . . Oh well . . . '

Mrs. Sutton, still muttering, went towards the kitchen and I stared after her as I picked up the telephone. Really, she had no right to make some of the remarks she did, and obviously felt she was duty bound to run all our lives. Ordinarily I found that comforting, but now she had my thoughts in a jumble as I picked up the telephone.

'Hello . . . yes?' I asked, hesitantly, hardly knowing what to say . . . 'Er . . . Mrs. Sutton?'

'You know very well who it is. That old horror Elliott keeps employed will have told you. Where is Elliott? I want to talk some things over with him.'

She used to be brisk and business-like, and I had always been aware of her competence, and had felt humbled by it. Now she sounded almost shrill, as though controlling deep anger. Was it true that she had wanted Elliott, but that he had not proposed to her? I knew very well now why he had avoided marriage, and I felt hollow as I wondered if Elliott had really cared for Stella Sutton. I remembered gaining the impression that there *had* been another woman in his life, but I had not connected that with Stella. Yet I felt that if I kow-towed to Stella Sutton, I would have lost the shred of dignity which still remained to me.

'My husband is in Zurich,' I told her, coolly.

There was a catch of breath, then the telephone was slammed down.

'Who was it?' asked Dympna, as I turned away.

'Elliott's previous secretary, Stella Sutton,' I said, reluctantly.

'Oh no, not again!' she said. 'I should have thought he'd be finished with all that now that he's married.'

Seeing the colour sweep my cheeks, she looked as though she could have bitten her tongue.

'All in the past, Berris dear,' she said. 'I'm sorry if I've put my foot in it. Elliott paid her some attention at one time, but he has chosen you. Don't worry about him.'

'It's all right,' I assured her. 'I can't . . . don't mind.'

I could not afford to mind.

Elliott returned home from Zurich the following day, and our time was taken up with making final preparations for Gerald's arrival. Nurse Selby had been interviewed and Elliott was satisfied that her references were excellent. She would not be able to come for the first week, but Ena Makin was sure she would be able to cope with anything that was required.

In the midst of all this activity, Dympna moved around calmly, her main interest being Helen, and I was glad to leave the baby in her care while I attended to all the small details, such as flowers in the bedroom and a good supply of toilet necessities and fresh linen.

Dympna pushed Helen in her pram on an errand to the village on Saturday morning, and did not arrive back home in time for lunch. I didn't particularly worry until after three o'clock. No doubt she had slipped into 'Irene's', our favourite tearoom for a quick lunch, or had called to see one of her friends. By three-fifteen I was growing alarmed as it was long past time for Helen's feed, and Dympna was meticulous about the baby's time table.

I went in search of Elliott who was working at his desk. He had been delighted by the calm way Dympna was taking the news of Gerald's return home, and by her obvious delight in Helen.

'It's wonderful,' he said to me, his eyes bright. 'Perhaps Dympna's whole problem has been one of frustrated motherhood! Now that she has the baby to care for, she is relaxing and can view everything much more rationally.'

I wished I could believe this.

'You don't agree, Berris? Can't you see she's so much better? You've done a wonderful job, darling.'

I felt the warm blood in my cheeks, pleased by the endearment. If only it could be so! Perhaps . . . perhaps Elliott would be so grateful that it would colour his attitude towards me. He might come to feel love for me . . . a form of love, at any rate.

But now as I went to find Elliott, I had a cold sick feeling of apprehension that something was very wrong.

‘She just hasn’t come home, Elliott,’ I told him. ‘I’m worried.’

‘Can’t she have gone somewhere? Haven’t you got any friends who would be so happy to see her and Helen, that they would forget the time?’

‘I’ll telephone everyone we know,’ I said. ‘I . . . I’ll be discreet.’

Elliott nodded, his mouth clamped rather hard, though I hated to see the worry in his eyes.

I drew a blank and we got into the car and drove to the village. Somewhere we might spot Helen’s pram outside a restaurant or shop.

The pram was there, outside the little cafe where Dympna and I often sat contentedly over a cup of coffee, and talked over any plans we had made. We had got to know the two women who ran the cafe and who lived above in a charming little flat. Both were keen helpers with the Red Cross work in which Dympna had always had an interest. Now Miss Patti Arnold had no idea of Dympna’s whereabouts, and went off to find Miss Mabel, who remembered seeing her coming in for a quick cup of coffee. She remembered it particularly since Dympna had brought Helen into the cafe, and Miss Mabel had admired the baby. Hearing her talk of how rounded Helen's tiny limbs had become, and how she had managed a smile for the elderly ladies caught at my heart, so that the full import was beginning to strike. Dympna had gone, and had taken my baby with her.

There was nothing to be gained from any of our friends and acquaintances, and Elliott and I were too worried to care any more about keeping up appearances. It was the friends who tried to put our fears at rest.

'I expect she's taken the bus,' Miss Patti said, 'and might even have left you a note, Mrs. Manley, if she forgot to tell you. She has probably taken her baby niece to see a friend. She's so proud of that baby!'

'I know,' I said, dismally. I was thinking of Dympna's mental state. I was sure she was convincing herself, at times, that the baby belonged to her!

'I'll ring round some of her friends who live a few miles away.'

Coming out of the cafe, Elliott turned up the street purposefully.

'Come on,' he said, briefly.

'Where to? Where are you going now, Elliott?'

'To the Police Station, or rather old Bob Holden's house. I'd better report Helen missing.'

'No! No . . . wait,' I said, feeling that we were rushing into unknown waters without due thought and consideration. Gradually I was realising that my baby was out of my control or protection, but I felt that Dympna's mind would have to be given a very severe jolt before Helen was in real danger from her. She would guard the baby with her life, but I had heard about people who could resort to . . . to killing as a way of protection. Was Dympna one of these? I felt we must do nothing to upset her, and a full-scale police hunt might not be the answer.

'Let's go home first, then ring up later when we've exhausted everything.'

'But we must think about the baby,' said Elliott.

His face was very white.

'You . . . *our* baby must come first, Berris,' he said, taking my hand. 'My sister isn't . . . isn't reliable and she has Helen.'

I had never seen him looking so white and grim-lipped.

'She won't harm Helen.'

'We can't take the risk. I feel responsible for putting your baby in this danger.'

'Let's go home, Elliott,' I said, tiredly. 'Let's think about what to do.'

Back home Mrs. Sutton was obviously waiting for us, coming forward with a look of bewildered curiosity.

'Miss Dympna rang up with a message for Mrs. Elliott,' she said, breathlessly.

'What was it?' I asked, while Elliott barked 'Well?' at the same time.

'She said not to worry about Helen. She was just taking care of her for a little while, and would write. Then . . . then she just hung up.'

Mrs. Sutton was obviously dying of curiosity, but Elliott just nodded and asked her to bring tea to the lounge while he guided me, pouring out a small glass of sherry from a decanter.

'This will warm you first of all,' he told me.

'I think I know where she has gone,' I said, sipping the sherry.

'Where?'

'To Highfield. She was asking me all about it. I think she has gone to avoid meeting Gerald, though I feel very angry that she has taken Helen. I don't blame her for going if she doesn't want to meet Gerald, but I *do* blame her for taking Helen, just because she's likely to miss her if she leaves her behind. The baby has given her a purpose in life, but she should know that Helen is mine . . . ours as far as she's concerned . . . and how much it would hurt both of us to take her away like that.'

The tears were beginning to come and Elliott put his arms round me.

'We can leave in an hour,' he told me. 'A few hours will get us well up the Motorway. Dympna may have gone by train . . .'

I hesitated. 'Leave it till tomorrow, Elliott. We're both very tired. Also, you've got to pick up Gerald.'

'Oh, lor' . . . Gerald!' he said. 'I forgot about him. This won't be a very welcoming gift for home-coming . . . the news that his wife won't even wait to see him. He keeps hoping she'll . . . she'll be completely better by now, but this shows that she is as bad as ever. I should have sought more expert help instead of trying out my own amateur psychology, and keeping the true state of affairs hidden from doctors who might have helped. It's my fault!'

'Don't blame yourself too much, Elliott. You did your best. I . . . I know you love Dympna. Gerald too.'

'He's a good soul and puts up with a lot.'

'We'll see him installed tomorrow, then I'll leave for the cottage. I'll take the small car. I . . . I think I might be able to talk to her myself.'

Elliott shook his head.

'I can't let you go alone.'

'I'll be all right. It's very much better this way if Dympna really *is* at the cottage. I'll be on home ground, don't forget. I'll pack a bag of extra clothes for Helen, and I'll try to see what Dympna has in mind. Believe me, if I feel I've got something I can't handle, I'll ring you immediately. In the meantime, you see to Gerald. Don't forget, this is going to set him back a bit, too.'

'I hadn't forgotten,' said Elliott bleakly.

I waited just long enough at Rosenwell to see Gerald Moryson comfortably installed in the sick room prepared for him. Mrs. Makin, wearing a white overall coat, briskly attended to him and it was only then that I learned she'd had some training as a nurse.

Gerald looked deathly pale, his noble head seeming too large for his thin body. Later Elliott told me he had taken the news about Dympna quietly, but the animation had gone from his face, leaving him looking very tired, the joy gradually going out of his face.

'I think he's only realising now that Dympna has changed,' said Elliott sadly. 'He has always believed it was only a temporary thing. Lor' . . . what a mess!'

'I'll talk to her, Elliott. You know, among my Cumbrian mountains, one does find the sort of peace which helps one to see a problem in its true perspective. Perhaps Dympna has been more clever than she realises by bolting for the cottage. Perhaps she'll be able to take a longer look at her life and see how wrong she has been.'

Elliott's dark eyes were grave, then he smiled and put his arms round me. I found my heart beating to suffocation point, but I could see that it was more for his own comfort than for mine.

'I wish it could be that easy, Berris,' he said.

'It might be. Don't give up.'

'The optimism of Youth. Sometimes I forget how young you are, then you give me a charming reminder.'

I felt vaguely cross. This was not quite what I wanted to hear.

I went upstairs to have a word with Gerald before I left, feeling that as Elliott's wife, I must extend this courtesy to him. When we had talked a little, however, I wondered if he guessed the truth of how things stood between Elliott and me. There was something about his eyes which seemed to see right into one's mind. I could not be comfortable with him, though he treated me with deference and respect.

'Are you comfortable, Gerald?' I asked him.

'As comfortable as my old bones will allow, my dear,' he smiled, rather ruefully.

'I'm sorry.'

I hung about awkwardly, not knowing how to talk to this man. I knew that he was so far above me intellectually that we might not have belonged to the same race.

'Well . . .' I turned away, hesitantly, and he smiled again.

'Don't worry, I'll soon be fighting fit again. I intend to make a new beginning, and I'm sure I can make Dympna realise this, and that I'm not angry with her. It was just a temporary upset, you know.'

'I know. I . . . I'll tell her if . . . if I find her, though I expect she'll come home on her own very soon . . . any time now. She's got to bring Helen back . . . you know.'

'She's a naughty girl taking your daughter away without permission.'

Was it my imagination or had he emphasized *your* daughter? Did he know my baby was not Elliott's? Feeling uncomfortable, I bade him goodbye and left the room thankfully.

Then I hurried to pick up my case with its few necessities, and the other case with extra things for Helen. I was so sure I would find Dympna at the cottage, and already I was planning how long we could stay there, just the three of us, until Dympna came to terms with herself, and her life. How long would that take? Would it be possible at all?

It seemed strange to be driving north again, and I could not help reflecting on the changes which had occurred in little over a year, the greatest of all being in myself. I felt as though I had aged ten years in one, though a glance at my own reflection showed that the ten years had brought assets rather than the reverse. I was better groomed, better clothed, better fed and a great deal more self-assured. On the other side of the coin, I seemed to have acquired many more problems. Then I had only one, the baby who was now my beloved daughter. Thinking about Helen encouraged me to put my foot down on the pedal, and I drove faster, though with care, over the next sixty-odd miles.

I came off the motorway at Scotch Corner and began the slower drive to Penrith, then along the narrow winding roads to Highfield. It had grown dark, but the night sky was always specially lovely to me, as it hung over the towering fells of North Lakeland. The sky was a vast expanse of blue velvet, lit by an almost full moon. The blazing gems of the stars were matched only by those picked up in the car headlights, the eyes of the sheep resting contentedly on the grassy verge of the hill road, or ambling from the road itself as I drove towards them. Here and there I saw the glow of lights from cottage windows, and in spite of the task which lay ahead, I felt a warm glow of well-being.

I was home.

There were no glowing lights from my cottage window, and for a long moment I felt a keen sense of disappointment. I had been wrong, and Dympna had not come to the cottage after all. She had somewhere of her own to hide. Elliott had telephoned her own home, and there had been no reply, but that did not mean she wasn't there. No doubt she had been cunning enough not to answer the telephone.

I parked the car and looked on my key-ring for the cottage key. It was too late to bother Mrs. Shorrock, but there was sure to be tins in the larder, and I could make a quick snack.

Then a thought occurred which made me hurry to open the car door. I always went to bed earlier at Highfield, and perhaps Dympna had also developed this habit. She was sure to be up early each morning to attend to Helen.

Hurrying up to the door I let myself in, and almost immediately I saw that I was correct. Dympna was here. The baby's shawl lay draped over a chair, and on a cabinet a small pile of clean nappies and 'baby-gros' had been dumped rather carelessly, no doubt waiting to be taken upstairs to the bedroom. In the kitchen I saw a milk bottle sticking out of a pan of water, and an empty tin of baby food thrown into the sink tidy.

Suddenly I couldn't wait any longer to see my baby and rushed upstairs to the small bedrooms, going first of all to my own bedroom where all was tidy, then into the spare room where I saw that a bed for Helen had been improvised out of a clothing basket, while Dympna was obviously using the bed . . . or *had* been using the bed. Now the bedroom was empty and, in fact, the whole house was empty. Where were they? I wondered. Had she, somehow, got wind of what I had in mind and had picked up the baby and fled again?

The hard lump which had been in my heart since Dympna took Helen away began to break up, and I found myself crying helplessly, even as I picked up a small boottee from among the blankets lining the clothes basket. I didn't care if I never saw Dympna again. I had not believed she was everything Elliott had feared in her, and had led her husband such a dance.

For the first time I began to see just what sort of a life she had led Gerald. She was an unstable woman who had almost killed her husband and herself, and had shown no remorse that she had made an invalid of a gentle, cultured man who had had the depth of character to see it in its true perspective, and to be willing to make excuses for her, and to hope she would throw off her madness and once again be the girl he married. He must be a saint, I thought. How awful for Elliott, knowing and loving Gerald as his oldest and dearest friend, yet seeing his life ruined by his sister.

And that sister now had *my* baby. I had been so confident that she would be here, and I could handle her, I had managed to persuade Elliott. I had encouraged him to put Gerald before Helen. Now I regretted that. Now nothing seemed to matter but getting my baby back, and I sat helplessly on

Dympna's bed, and let the hot scalding tears roll down my cheeks. If I could have put back the clock, I would have done so, though it meant losing the little bit I'd had of Elliott.

I had *nothing* of Elliott, I reminded myself in my depression. He had not wanted me. He had only wanted a nurse for his sister. And I had sacrificed my baby to her.

I had no idea how long I sat there, though my feet had gone leaden and I shook with cold. Then I heard the sound of voices, and the baby crying, and the door opened loudly downstairs. I could hear Dympna's charming voice and the more strident tones of Mrs. Shorrock, even as Helen's wails grew in strength.

Slowly and stiffly I rose from sitting on the bed, and made my way downstairs to confront the two older women.

'I knew you'd come,' Dympna said, simply.

'Och, my poor Berris,' Mrs. Shorrock

began, but I brushed her aside and went forward, cat-like, towards Dympna, wanting to scratch and claw at her. Part of my mind was registering primitive emotions and behaviour, but I didn't care.

'You horror!' I said to her. 'Give me my baby . . .'

'But Berris! Darling! You know I'd *never* hurt her. You don't know why I took her . . .'

'I *do* know. You want to steal her from me, that's why.'

My baby was screaming now, beating the air with tiny fists.

'Och, you need to calm down, Berris . . . er . . . Mrs. Manley,' said Mrs. Shorrock, taking Helen from me.

I was too tired to hold her, and I could see Dympna staring at me, her eyes wide with hurt and fright. I had never been anything but gentle and understanding with her. She had come to expect it.

'I . . . I'm sorry, Berris,' she said, 'as I say, you don't understand, and I could not explain before. But I can now.'

'No explanations or anything till morning,' said Mrs. Shorrock, firmly. 'Can't you see the lass is dead on her feet, Mrs. Moryson? She'll be a different girl after a good night's sleep. You can all talk tomorrow.'

I was deathly weary. Helen was safe, and Mrs. Shorrock looking after her. Like an automaton I nodded, and went towards my own bedroom, where I pulled off my clothes and crawled between the sheets. What a good place it was to be, and how pedestrian my bedroom seemed after the one I had been given at Rosenwell, yet every inch was mine, and every inch breathed peace rather than prosperity.

Mrs. Shorrock brought me hot milk laced with brandy, which warmed me, and she told me that Helen was now fast asleep and would no doubt stay 'sound' until morning. Gratefully I let go and felt the warmth of sleep stealing over me.

7

Next morning I woke early, wondering what I should do. I could either get up now, dress my baby, and take her straight back to Rosenwell, or follow my inclinations and stay on here at Highfield, but ask Dympna to leave. My inclinations were to remain in the only home which I felt was entirely mine. I rang up Rosenwell, and left a message that Dympna and Helen were safe, and that I'd get in touch.

I felt as though the experiment had failed. I was not qualified to deal with a woman like Dympna, and Elliott had been quite wrong to ask it of me. I thought of Rosenwell with a lump in my throat. I had begun to love it, too, but there was no real love for me in return. My relationship with Elliott was only a business one, when I got down to brass tacks as they say, and I'd had enough of it. I had failed. Elliott must seek expert help and advice over his problem, even if he felt that a wrong step might ruin Dympna's chances of a reasonable life in the future. I sympathized. Until she stole my baby, I had been growing fond of her, but now my maternal instinct was uppermost, and nothing and nobody was going to put Helen at risk. Not even Elliott.

I thought of him numbly. I knew that I loved him and after the whole sorry mess had been cleared up from my point of view, I would still have a deep emptiness because of him. But he didn't care for me, and I had seen marriages stagger and founder with love on both sides. Ours had very little hope of a future when it was no marriage in the first place.

I forced myself to think rationally. If I stayed at Highfield, I would be back to the awful grind of having to earn a living for Helen and me. But Mrs. Shorrock might help by taking care of her during the day, if I earned enough to pay her well. I could get some sort of hotel job again. I'd do anything to make a life of independence for myself and my baby.

My mind made up, I went through to the kitchen. Dympna could take the car back to Rosenwell. I tried not to remember that other car she had driven . . . into a wall! Was I being irresponsible in throwing her out like this, and asking her to drive to a home she feared? Rightly or wrongly, she feared living with her husband, and that's what going back to Rosenwell might mean.

Again my head began to ache as I turned over all these problems. Elliott had no right to involve me in such an insoluble situation. Yet I had asked for it, I remembered fairly. He, himself, had seen the snags and had tried to back out. He had only gone through with it after I had convinced him I was capable of tackling it. I had done so in desperation, because of my own situation at the time, and that situation was unchanged if I came back to Highfield permanently.

Helen was stirring in her cot and I lifted her out quietly, carrying her into the kitchen to heat her milk. It was warm there, and I selected clean clothing from the pile I had found, and made my baby comfortable.

* * *

About an hour later Dympna appeared looking pale with blue smudges under her eyes, which made her look as though she had slept badly.

'I didn't hear you get up. Helen usually wakes me,' she said, 'but I didn't hear her this morning. You must have picked her up before she yelled.'

'I *am* her mother,' I reminded her, quietly.

I stared at her coldly, and she pushed her hair away from her forehead.

'Is there any coffee? Perhaps that will make me feel more human. Don't look at me like that, Berris. I know you think

I . . . I more or less *stole* Helen, but it just isn't true. I had to do something to keep Gerald away from her . . . from even *looking* at her. I didn't want his evil eyes on her. Somehow I felt that even his presence around her was a threat to her . . . her purity, and that he'd pollute the very air she breathed.'

My mouth went dry. Dympna sat not a yard away from me, having poured herself a cup of unsweetened black coffee. She looked so normal, yet here she was saying the most crazy things. I'd had no experience of mental illness, but somehow I expected people who were affected by it to *look* different, yet here she was, the same quiet gentle woman I had known at Rosenwell.

Deep down I felt a strange fear and dread of her, the sort of fear which builds up when facing the unknown. I could not argue with her rationally. I could only placate her, and somehow or other get hold of Elliott, and ask him to come for her. I could tell him our bargain was at an end, and if I owed him anything, I had well and truly paid it over the past couple of days with all the horror I was going through.

But I would have to arrange things so that Dympna was never left alone with Helen. Somehow I would have to explain to Mrs. Shorrock that she was not to be trusted.

She was pouring herself a second cup, having peeped at Helen who was sleeping in the basket-cot.

'Isn't she an angel?' asked Dympna. 'Just think . . . I might have had a daughter like her if . . . if Gerald had not murdered my baby before it was born. Sometimes I'm glad he did. I don't think I could have loved my own child so much, knowing that it was also Gerald's child. How could I have been sure of keeping it free of *his* evil, when it had *his* blood in its veins.'

I stared at her fascinated, listening to the calm quiet voice saying these words of hatred. Her eyes only reflected a great sadness, as though she had suffered a great deal over a long time.

'That's a terrible thing to say, Dympna,' I told her.

She knelt down by the kitchen fire, rubbing her hands as though they were full of cold, then threw some more logs on the fire, blowing the embers gently with the old brown bellows.

'I know, but it's true. Can I tell you about it, Berris? After all, you're my sister . . . or nearly . . . and I have no one-else I can tell. I tried to make Elliott understand once upon a time, but he obviously thought I was hysterical, or worse.'

I swallowed. Was it best to let her talk?

'All . . . all right,' I agreed, huskily, 'though I don't really feel qualified to help with your private affairs, Dympna.'

'I've got to talk to someone! I couldn't . . . before . . . '

My heart leapt, startled, at the sudden strength of her tone. She had shouted so loudly that Helen's hands flew up and her tiny face crumpled, so that Dympna immediately knelt beside her, shooing her gently.

'There . . . there, my pet. Aunt Dympna forgot to be quiet.'

Slowly the baby's eyes grew heavy, and she slept again.

'Say on,' I said. I might as well get it over.

'I was younger than you when I first met Gerald,' said Dympna, coming to sit beside me in front of the blazing logs. 'I hadn't bothered much with boys of my own age. They bored me. And I *had* been curious about Gerald for some time, since Elliott was always talking about him. He was a wonderful man, and rather tragic since he had lost his young wife, and though his work seemed to fit the mould of a dry-as-dust professor, Elliott kept talking about how good-looking he was.

'Even that had not prepared me for Gerald's sheer beauty. Well . . . you've seen him, Berris. Can you imagine how he looked ten years younger, and before . . . before the accident? He reminded me of some marvellous old Biblical paintings, and I was terribly awed by him. Later he began to pay me special attention, and to make me feel important, I fell in love with him. It was one of those total loves which seems to embrace everything.

'I suppose if Father had been alive, I wouldn't have married Gerald.' Dympna's voice grew bitter. 'For one thing, I . . . I wouldn't have had the money . . .'

'Oh, but surely . . . ' I began, and she stared at me stonily.

'I wouldn't have had the money,' she repeated. 'It wasn't apparent at first. Therein lies his devilry. He made me wait for that, saying that he only wanted me all to himself to begin with. I saw later that . . . that he never wanted a child. He wanted everything for himself.'

Dympna stared into the fire, and threw on another log.

'It was insidious at first . . . just small teasing remarks . . . gentle laughter . . . a tiny mistake put right. Yet can you imagine what it feels like for that to go on and on? One begins to feel stupid without knowing why. Day in and day out, the lightest of ridicule, the gentlest of rebukes, increasing little by little, yet so hard to get hold of. I tried to tell Elliott at first, but I could find nothing really concrete to complain about. When I gathered myself together and tried to explain things logically, it seemed as though I were being neurotic, and Gerald's earnest concern, then indulgent sympathy always had Elliott looking with concern . . . at him!'

I found that I was beginning to listen. Something about this story from Dympna was beginning to ring true. For the first time I was seeing that she could have a point of view.

'Go on,' I urged her.

She turned to look at me, and after a while she nodded as though accepting that I understood.

'It went on so long that it became a way of life. I *became* the sort of fumbling bumbling woman he was trying to create. In private he no longer pretended innocence and began to belittle everything I tried to do. And a person with Gerald's wonderful brain can find a million ways to do this. In fact, he seemed to find his greatest enjoyment in working out new ways of destroying any confidence I tried to keep.

'Sometimes, at night, I would lie awake and will myself back into the past. I would remember things I had accomplished and tell myself I was still that same girl. I could still do all those things if I wished. Then in the morning Gerald would be there, and I was reduced to a jelly, shivering and helpless, yet a small core in me refusing to give up completely. I was *not* a jelly. I was a woman, with a brain and a certain competence. He would *not* take it away.'

Dympna's face had become white and drawn, yet I could see that small core in her. It was the same quality which I knew was in Elliott, something indestructible.

'Gerald was doing some sort of involved research, and writing it all up for publication, but he needed money. I had already made over fairsized sums to him, but he needed more, and more, and more. Yet always I held on to the bulk. I wanted a child. I knew my feelings for him were dead, so dead that I could not even hate him. When I became pregnant he was furious, and the cruelty of mind he inflicted began to be less subtle and more deliberate. For a while this was easier to fight, like an enemy seen, not unseen, then one morning I tripped over my housecoat as I ran out of the bedroom with my eyes full of tears, and I fell downstairs. I lost my baby.'

'I . . . I'm sorry,' I said. 'Truly sorry.'

'Oh, I made myself get over it, and it brought new feeling to me. Now I began to hate him. It was better than feeling nothing at all.'

I stared at her, fascinated. The colour

had begun to fill her cheeks.

'I suppose I must have gone out of my mind for a time, but when I found out that Gerald's first wife met with an accident, and he practically told me it was no accident, but just 'a little bit of help towards some prosperity', I began to get frightened. Who could help me? Who would believe that the noble, gentle, cultured man who was Gerald Moryson was really a fiend, and could be a murderer? I was afraid they would think that I had lost my reason, yet I knew it was a hint from Gerald that my own destruction would be very advantageous to him, and he had only married me because I was an heiress.

'Gradually I was learning that . . . that he hated women.'

I shivered as we sat silent for a moment, though I knew now that Dympna was telling me the truth. *That* was what I had felt about Gerald. He hated women . . . he hated *me*. I remembered the flash of something I had seen in his eyes, and I knew now what it was.

'I asked you if he was homosexual,' I reminded her.

'But he wasn't! He was quite normal. He just hated women's minds, not their bodies.'

'I wonder what I had sensed about him,' I mused.

'I felt that my life was over, anyway,' said Dympna. 'Sooner or later he would get his own way. He would drive me to taking my own life. Then I began to feel determined again, that he would not get away with it. I would end my life . . . it was just a burden to me . . . but he would not prey on any other woman. Nor would he reap the benefit of *my* money.

'I laid my plans carefully, and waited until an opportunity presented itself. Sooner or later we would have to go to town, and he would ask me to drive. It had happened before. I had nothing prepared. I knew my affairs were in order, and I could not care less how

Gerald's stood. There was a high wall not a hundred yards from our home. It was built to prop up subsidence, and just far enough away for me to get up a bit of speed in the car. I put my foot down and drove straight for it, only the speed was not great enough, or the car was stronger than I thought.

'I know now that I must have been out of my mind, and that was accepted by the authorities. Gerald was severely injured, as you know, and I got off more lightly. I told . . . told as much as I could remember of what had happened.

'Later I pretended that I was too ashamed to face my husband because I almost killed him, but I told Elliott the truth, that I hated Gerald. I didn't want to go near him, and tried to get Elliott to take me away, and not allow Gerald near me. But now Gerald hates me worse than ever, and would do anything to injure me. That's why he tries to blacken me to Elliott. It takes away my one prop. If he finds out how . . . how much I love Helen, he would find some way of harming her.'

Suddenly she was sobbing, dry harsh sobs. 'I had to get her away, Berris. Don't you see? He mustn't even see her.'

'Ssh . . . ssh!'

I was rocking her in my arms while she cried like a small child. Yet I knew that here, at last, all the misery and evil treatment by Gerald Moryson was being washed out of her. I let her cry and cry, and soon she lay back, tired, and sobbing quietly.

'That hasn't happened to me for years,' she said.

'I'll make some tea,' I said. 'I think you'll feel better now, and if it matters, I believe every word you have told me, and I'll see that Elliott does, too.'

'You're a wonderful sister,' said Dympna.

But not for long, I thought, sadly.

8

Now that Dympna had told me all about her marriage to Gerald Moryson, I felt that I had new problems on my hands. I had intended to ask her to go back home, either to her own home or Rosenwell, but now I felt that it would be better for her to stay with me until the problem of Gerald had been resolved. She was not going back to him if I could help it.

I wrote a brief note to Elliott telling him she was with me, and we would not be returning for the moment. Dympna's eyes showed fear when she came in and found me addressing the letter.

'Don't tell Elliott. Please don't tell him,' she pleaded. 'Not for another day or two. Give me that at least.'

'But he's worried about you,' I protested, and wondered whether to tell her I had already phoned Rosenwell on the morning after I arrived. 'Elliott will want to know you are safe and well.'

'But he'll tell Gerald, and they'll make me return . . . to Gerald. I'm afraid of him getting better and forcing me to live with him again. Don't you see? I was almost crazy before, else I would never have tried to do such . . . such a stupid thing with the car. I . . . I suppose by rights I should be in jail, but Elliott sorted something out with our solicitor, and I had to go to some sort of clinic for examination. I suppose I got away with it because neither of us was killed, nor did it involve another person . . . '

She babbled on nervously, biting her lip.

'It's all in the past, Dympna,' I said. 'Calm down, dear. You can stay here, if you like, until you decide what to do. Why don't you divorce Gerald? I'm sure you have grounds . . . mental cruelty for one thing. And anyway, you don't *have* to live with him if you don't want. He can't force you . . . '

'Can't he?'

Her eyes were wide but still frightened, and I was amazed at how young she really was. She didn't seem to know very much about her rights.

'No, he can't. Not in this day and age.'

She turned away and stood very still for a while, and I saw that she was crying quietly again.

'I . . . I didn't know,' she said at length. 'It's like being allowed out of prison. I . . . we were brought up to think of marriage as being something sacred which went on until death. The fact that I *could* live apart from my husband seemed impossible . . . unless he were in hospital, that is. I . . . I thought he had jurisdiction over me, and that wherever I went, he would always be able to find me. I knew I was safe while he was ill, but soon he'll be well again.'

'And you can thank God for it,' I told her. 'What a crazy thing to do.'

'I know,' she said tiredly. 'I can see

that now, but I had no level-headed sister, then, to keep me seeing things in their true perspective, and Elliott could never believe anything against Gerald. How will we ever be able to make him see my point of view?'

'I'll make him see it,' I told her, grimly.

'But it's putting you in an awful position. I couldn't make trouble between you and Elliott . . . I just couldn't! There's the baby to be considered . . . '

'Don't think of it now,' I told her.

Sooner or later I might have to put Dympna straight about Elliott and me.

* * *

I didn't know what Elliott would say when I finally heard from him, and I didn't worry for the moment. I was too busy settling into the cottage again, and going for long lovely walks with Dympna and Helen.

'No wonder you love it all, Berris,'

Dympna said as we stood in pale bright sunshine and allowed the scented hill air to blow freshness into our hair and our lungs.

'What a pity Elliott can't just retire and come to live here with you. But I expect he'll always want to keep Rosenwell. I know he's bound to love Helen, but he'll be hoping for a son next time . . . '

'There will be no next time,' I said, thoughtlessly, and she whirled round to stare at me.

'What do you mean, Berris?'

'Oh nothing, dear. Just one of those meaningless things people say from time to time.'

'No. You meant it.'

She came to walk beside me, and took my arm.

'I . . . I wondered now and again. Have I come between you and Elliott in any way?'

'No, of course you haven't.'

I couldn't look at her, and I knew she didn't believe me. We walked in silence for a while, then Dympna said rather bitterly.

'I'm a fool. I should have known that sort of thing would happen. You . . . you've probably quarrelled about me. I wouldn't have had that happen for the world. Look, Berris dear, I'll leave in the morning, just so long as you stay here with Helen for a week or two. Try to make Elliott see you need a rest with the baby, and go back home after Gerald goes. Don't take Helen back to Rosenwell while Gerald is there. But do make Elliott realize you still love him. Don't break up your marriage because . . . because of my experiences, Berris. I would feel terrible about that.'

'Don't worry so.' I tried to pacify her, then somehow I was fed up with all the sham and pretence. She was going to have to know some time.

'As a matter of fact, there is no real marriage to break up. Elliott and I . . . we've never really had a proper marriage as such. So you can stop worrying about Helen. I've decided to stay here with her now. Somehow we'll manage, and you can remain here till you feel you'd like to get on with your life again.'

She looked horrified!

'But . . . but you *can't* just leave Elliott like that. You can't break up his life, for me.'

'It isn't just for you. Elliott doesn't love me, Berris. He . . . he only married me to give my child a name. I'm sorry you're having to find out like this but you have to know some time . . . '

'You mean you *lived* together . . . Elliott! . . . and . . . '

'No, not Elliott. It . . . it was a young student I knew . . . an American. Oh, Dympna, I really am sorry, but you *have* to find out the truth. Helen is *my* child, not Elliott's. I . . . I'm afraid she's not really your niece.'

Dympna had gone white with shock and I felt terrible. I should never have told her so soon on top of everything else. Every now and again I felt I was an older, mature woman, then I would do something which showed me how young and stupid I really was. This was one of those times.

'Come on, let's get home,' I said. 'It was stupid of me to tell you like that . . . '

'No . . . let me be by myself for a moment. Just leave me,' she said. 'I know you must be telling me the truth, but . . . but suddenly everything is strange and unreal. I . . . I'll have to get used to it. Let me walk a little way by myself.'

I hesitated, wondering desperately what to do. What if this had been the final straw for Dympna? What if she had now been given more than she could take?

'Don't go far, Dympna,' I pleaded. 'The mists can come down so quickly and you could get lost so easily. You're wearing light trousers, too, and that's the worst possible garment against the mists. They cling to your clothing, all damp and icy, and you become paralysed with cold in no time.'

'I'll take care,' she said, coldly. 'Just . . . just leave me. I have to think this out.'

I spent the most anxious afternoon in my whole life. More and more I was realizing that by blurting out the truth, as I had, I had not only shocked Dympna, but may have lost her trust, and even her friendship. Only now did I realize that it had become rather precious to me. I had enjoyed having a sister, while it lasted.

At last I saw Dympna coming home, her step firm and sure. I ran to the door to let her in, and a look at her face told me she had not forgiven me for the news I had just given her.

'Get out of your damp clothes,' I told her. 'I've got some soup ready.'

'I'm quite warm,' she said, briefly, 'but there are one or two things I have to know.'

I felt my cheeks colour with shame at the direct look she gave me.

'Such as what?'

'Such as why Elliott married you when you were expecting someone else's child, unless he was deeply in love with you . . . '

'He wasn't and isn't. He had his own reasons.'

She stared at me thoughtfully.

'You know Stella Sutton, don't you, Berris?' she asked.

'Yes.'

'Was it because of her?'

'What do you mean?'

'I used to believe he was in love with her. She always acted as though . . . as though there was something between them.'

I said nothing. Perhaps this had been true. Perhaps Elliott had not wanted to marry a girl he had fallen in love with, since he didn't want children. Perhaps that's why Stella seemed to have power over him, yet accepted a life apart from Elliott. She would not want a 'problem' child any more than Elliott.

Yet if he knew the real truth behind Dympna's odd behaviour, and realized that in fact, she was emotionally as strong as a horse, things could be different for him. Anyone less stable would have folded up long ago. Would he then regret not having married Stella? Would he want a quick divorce in order to get on with living his own life?

I had thought I wanted to stay at Highfield, well away from Elliott, but now knives seemed to cut into my heart at the thought of a final break.

'She had a child, didn't she? I sometimes wondered if . . . though Elliott isn't like that.'

'No, it wasn't Elliott's child,' I assured her. 'That much I *do* know.'

'How do you know?'

She was swift to question me.

'Because he didn't want children . . . at least he didn't then . . . '

'Because of me? Because he believed me to be unstable?'

My face must have given her the answer because she turned away again.

'How little we really know about

. . . about the people closest to us,' she said sadly, 'the people we love. I knew that Elliott was concerned about my nerves, but I never knew that by keeping quiet, and enduring my life with Gerald as far as possible, I was already spoiling Elliott's life. I never knew that by trying to take the law into my own hands, I was confirming all he believed of me.'

The tears were back in her voice as she walked up and down, then she suddenly turned on me.

'But in one way I'm glad. I could never stand that Sutton woman. But you've been like my own sister, and I can't stop loving the baby just because she's yours and not Elliott's. I thought I could, and for a moment I hated you when you told me the truth. But I can't. Berris, I'm sure Elliott loves you. Please don't break with him. Try to make it up to him for all this. Try to love him a little . . . '

The last remark caught me unawares, and my face crumpled.

'Shut up!' I cried. 'Oh, *do* shut up. You don't know what you're saying.'

'You *do* love him,' she said. 'That's it, isn't it? You love Elliott.'

'Yes I do, but he doesn't give a fig for me. It was a . . . a business arrangement. I was to be his wife and help to run Rosenwell till you came home, then try my best to get you better, so that you and Gerald . . . '

'Yes, I see,' she said, quietly. 'I see it all now.'

'Only you aren't going back to Gerald, not ever. I don't care if Elliott hates me for it, but we're going to tell him the truth, Dympna. Tomorrow we are going to pack up and go back to Rosenwell, and you're going to face that fiend. We'll face him together, because I can bear out what you've said about him. It's true he hates women. I could *feel* it in him. He hates both of us.'

'Not tomorrow,' said Dympna. 'Give me more time. I can't face it just yet.'

'It must be done soon. The longer you put it off, the harder it will be. But we'll tell Elliott the truth and leave it to him. Afterwards, if you want to come back here, then we'll come. It will be my home anyway, mine and Helen's.'

But Dympna had said nothing and I could see the rigid fear settling on her face again. I was going to have trouble in getting her back to Rosenwell, but it was the only thing to do.

I was sure of that.

We left Highfield for Rosenwell the following day, though I only packed those things which were necessary for Helen. I didn't know how long it would take to sort out the mess between Dympna and Gerald, and the further resultant mess between Elliott and me, though I didn't suppose that would take long. Elliott must have had it all cut and dried else he would never have offered me marriage. The ties which bound us were not likely to be very tight.

I thought about Dympna sitting quietly beside me. There was a difference in her now, and I knew that part of that difference was serenity, and resolution. She had reached rock bottom over what Gerald Moryson could do to her, and knowing that he had no real hold over her, or one which could not be broken, had given her the incentive to make a positive break with him. Somehow the fear which had bound her to him was now broken, and with that came new courage.

She was holding Helen in her arms while I drove, and I knew that she loved my baby very much. Her biggest hatred of Gerald had come when his cruelty destroyed their baby, his own child, though she knew that his only desire was for her money, and he had no intention of sharing that with anyone, even a child.

As the miles were eaten up I was amazed by her quietness and courage. If her stomach was being eaten by nerves, as mine was, she did not show it, and it was left to me to feel sick with apprehension as we neared Rosenwell. We stopped at a small café for a quick meal and to change the baby, and I took the opportunity of phoning Mrs. Sutton. I learned that Elliott had been in Italy, but was due home at any time. Gerald was still installed in the sick room, with Nurse Selby looking after him. Mrs. Sutton did not approve of Nurse Selby and seemed to think that a nice man like Mr. Gerald deserved someone better.

'Miss Dympna is with me,' I told her, 'but she's very tired, so please don't mention to anyone that she's on her way home. She can just slip up to bed, and we'll sort it out tomorrow.'

'Very good, Miss Berris . . . Mrs. Elliott,' said the housekeeper. 'It's getting late. I'll stay up and help with the baby. She must be tired, poor little love.'

I had not realized it was so late, but now I could see the Motorway cafe was, in fact, closing and we still had some distance to go. I remembered that Elliott and I had done the journey in two days. Coming north I had just driven on and on, but it had taken us longer with Helen.

'She's sleeping,' I said. 'We'll be as quiet as we can.'

I didn't want to face Elliott that night, and was relieved that he was not home, then wondered, uneasily, where he *was*, since he had not as yet arrived home. Had he gone to see Stella Sutton? The old jealousy left a nasty taste in my mouth, but when I eventually crawled into bed, I was too tired to care, and slept as though drugged.

Next morning I woke, feeling heavy and unrefreshed. The telephone rang after I came down to breakfast, finding Dympna there before me looking neat, though I could see that her face was white and rather set again. Now that she was near her ordeal, she was having to draw on reserve strength.

I answered the telephone, my heart leaping when I heard Elliott's voice.

'Mrs. Sutton? I'm just going up north . . .'

'It's me . . . Berris,' I said, and heard his in-drawn breath.

'So you're home! I was wondering when you were going to think of coming back. It might interest you to know I'm half-way up the Motorway towards Highfield.'

'Oh Elliott! I . . . I'm sorry . . . ' I said, lamely.

'It doesn't matter,' he said. 'Is Dympna with you?'

'Yes.'

'Well, that's something at any rate.'

There was a sudden lightness in his voice.

'Luckily I rang before I had gone too far. I'll come straight home now. I shan't stop for lunch, other than coffee and a sandwich. See you in a couple of hours . . . '

I had decided that we would not disturb Gerald Moryson until Elliott arrived, and could see Mrs. Sutton mulling this over. To her mind it wasn't natural that Miss Dympna had not hurried off to make a fuss of Mr.

Gerald, and him such a nice gentleman, too. I saw Nurse Selby, and asked her to say nothing to him about our return, and when Elliott arrived home, we would all go in and see Gerald together. It would be a nice surprise for him, agreed Nurse Selby.

When Elliott arrived some two hours later, I found my heart beating to suffocation point when I heard his voice in the hall, and went out to meet him. He strode forward and I found myself crushed against his chest, then he kissed Dympna and took Helen in his arms.

'Where have you all been?' he demanded. 'Didn't it occur to you that I might miss you? I hadn't realized how much!'

'There's no need to pretend, Elliott,' I said, quietly. 'Dympna knows.'

'Knows?'

He stared at me, then at his sister, his eyes puzzled.

'All about . . . everything,' I said, impatiently. 'After you've had something to eat, and . . . and a bath and change of clothes, we would like to go and see Gerald, together. Dympna wants to come with both of us, then when you've heard what she has to say in front of Gerald, and not behind his back, I think you'll realize the true state of affairs with regard to her marriage. Dympna isn't sick, Elliott. She's fine, but she has the problem of her marriage to resolve.'

'Berris has . . . has made me see things absolutely straight,' said Dympna, quietly, and Elliott looked from one to the other of us and nodded, as though accepting that everything was now in perspective.

'You've done a good job, Berris,' he said, quietly.

'Fulfilled my part of the bargain,' I said, but he was already on his way upstairs to bath and change, while Mrs. Sutton prepared a quick meal for him. He looked tired, and I thought that perhaps he'd had little sleep because of his recent trip to Italy.

An hour later, however, he was much refreshed, and all three of us made our way towards Gerald's room, where Elliott asked Nurse Selby to go down to the kitchen and share a pot of tea with Mrs. Sutton.

Then for the first time in months, Gerald and Dympna Moryson were face to face.

Again I watched the strange flicker in Gerald Moryson's eyes when he caught sight of his wife, though I knew now how to interpret it. He hated Dympna with an intense hatred, no doubt increased by the fact that she had almost killed him, and had been responsible for weeks of lying on a hospital bed. For this I conceded he had a case, but I knew now that there had been hatred in him even before that.

The look was gone in a moment, and he was smiling at her with just the right amount of eagerness and loving welcome. I had to remind myself what he was really like, and that the looks of a saint masked the evil of his true nature.

'Dympna! My dearest! I thought I was *never* going to see you again. Why didn't you come and see me when you were able? You must have known I wouldn't be angry with you, my darling, and there is no need to be afraid of me, or shy . . .'

I felt Dympna tremble beside me, and put out a hand to steady her, taking hold of her arm. Elliott had gone over to the bed, a smile of relief on his face.

'You see, Gerald, how things can work out well after all? I've had a word with the doctor, and he says there's no reason why you can't try to walk a bit further now. I didn't know you were actually managing to walk at all, but he says you were getting very good in hospital with one of these walking aids. I've had a word with Nurse Selby, and she is going to give you massage. You should be fighting fit in another week or two.'

Gerald glared at Elliott, then again he came up smiling.

'Sometimes the hospital authorities try so hard, my dear Elliott,' he said. 'Didn't they mention that I had a set-back because of their misplaced optimism? The doctor in charge of my case . . . Dr. Leigh . . . understands this, and you should have talked to him. Ill-advised treatment can do untold harm.'

Elliott nodded. It was wise to let Gerald take his own time, especially now that Dympna was back home again.

But Dympna had come forward to face Gerald.

'I'm sorry I caused your accident, Gerald,' she said clearly. 'It was a mad thing to do, and I suppose I was a little mad in those days, but I've got my sanity back now, thanks to Berris.'

The gentle brown eyes swivelled in my direction and I could see the yellow flash in them again. I shivered, praying for courage for Dympna.

'I thought I *had* to live with you, that the law required me to live with you, or

. . . or I would lose every penny I possess to you. Come to think of it, I believe it was you who encouraged me to think so.'

'What?'

Elliott had turned to stare at Dympna, his face pale again, and I recognized his look of endurance. It was the one which said he had an unstable sister, and must learn to live with the fact. I quickly went to his side.

'Let her speak, Elliott,' I whispered. 'She's got to get it over with. Let her say what she feels.'

He looked at me doubtfully, but my eyes were on Gerald Moryson. The soft gentleness was beginning to leave him.

'What . . . what's all this, my dear? What bee have you been getting in your bonnet, and dear Berris helping you? Really, when you girls get together . . .'

'You know very well what bee, Gerald,' Dympna said, quietly, and firmly. 'The bee which has been making my life Hell for years. I married you because I loved you, and it took a long time for you to kill that love, Gerald, but you managed it. You did it very cleverly, undermining my self-confidence, gradually making me believe myself a creature of lower and lower intelligence, though perhaps Elliott will remember that at one time I was nothing of the kind, nor am I now . . .'

'But of *course* you aren't, darling. Whatever gave you . . .'

'That idea? You did, Gerald. You criticized every statement, every opinion I had, and questioned every decision I made. You worked on my mind till I hardly knew what day it was. My brains were just a jumbled mess, and through my mind, you attacked my body so that I lost my child . . . our child . . . yours as well as mine. But you didn't care. It just gave more credence to the picture you presented to the public . . . even to my own brother . . . that the miscarriage had unhinged me and that you were having a terrible life with . . . with an unbalanced woman.'

Gerald was looking round helplessly, his hands held out in appeal to Elliott, who was now very red in the face.

'For God's sake, Dympna!' he cried. 'If this is all you can say to Gerald . . . And you, Berris. Is *this* what you meant by saying she is well now!'

My heart sank when I saw his anger and disappointment, but I dug my nails into my palms and faced both of them.

'It's the truth she's telling . . . *listen* to her!' I cried.

'What about your last wife, Gerald?' Dympna was saying. 'She committed suicide. I tried to, as well, and take you with me so that you could never put another woman through the Hell you mapped out for me.'

She turned to Elliott.

'Look at me, Elliott. Don't you remember what I was like? Don't you remember? If I was happily married to a saintly man such as *he* claims to be, there would be no need for all this. We would have been delighted with one another. But all he wants is my money to carry on his research projects, and he doesn't want to risk going to prison by popping me off, even in some sort of accident. That would be too humane for a sadistic mind like his. No, he has to do it slowly, turn my mind inside out so that I do the job for him. He will just be unfortunate Gerald who's had the bad luck to pick *another* unbalanced woman. No one will remember that they were both wealthy. He's such a gentle, charming man everyone will be sorry for him.' She turned fiercely to Gerald. 'I wish I'd made a job of you! And to think I haven't even managed to cripple you!'

Deliberately Dympna had goaded him and now the snake which lived in Gerald Moryson seemed to leap out of him, and we watched the handsome, charming face crumple into a hideous thing, mouthing obscenities as he tried to claw his wife.

'Bitch! Rotten little . . . That *you* should try to kill *me* . . . *me*! How dare a stupid ignorant nonentity like *you* try to harm *me* . . . '

He writhed in the bed as Elliott held him, ringing the bell for the nurse, who came hot foot up the stairs, and stared at us all in indignation.

'Really . . . how could you upset my patient! Don't upset yourself, dear Mr. Moryson . . . '

'Be quiet, woman!' said Elliott.

I had never seen such a set mask on his face as he turned to me.

'Take Dympna to her room and ring for the doctor,' he said. 'I'll see to . . . to Gerald.'

Dympna was sobbing again, quietly, and trembling with all the effort. She was wonderfully brave, I thought, to know that somewhere a wild animal had lurked in Gerald and she had deliberately tempted it to the surface.

'Come on, my dear,' I said. 'Leave things to Elliott now.'

9

I never did find out just what happened to Gerald Moryson. The doctor came and a few hours later he was taken downstairs into an ambulance, and driven away. I presumed Elliott had arranged for him to be admitted to a nursing home . . . perhaps the same one . . . until he was completely better. I also suspected that he was far from being the helpless invalid he pretended, and that no doubt he would be back to living his own life again, but without Dympna.

As soon as possible she intended to sue for divorce, and this did happen, though it was all in the future. On that grim day I could only see vaguely that Dympna would one day be free again, to enjoy her life, and to be happy and confident in herself. But for the moment she was shaking with nervous exhaustion, her emotions in tatters.

I asked the doctor to have a look at her after seeing to Gerald, and he was full of kindness and sympathy, putting her to bed with a sedative.

'She needs complete rest,' he said to Elliott and me. 'A holiday perhaps, well away from here.'

'Highfield,' I suggested. 'In Cumbria,' I added turning to the doctor who thought that was a fine idea. 'Dympna has been there for a week already, and it seemed to do her good. I . . . I think we ought to go back there, Elliott, as soon as possible.'

He looked rather distracted.

'Can't she just stay here for a few days? There's so much I have to see to . . . arrangements to be made.'

'She's better away from all that,' I said, though in my heart I knew that I was the one who wanted to get away. I knew it was the end of my marriage, though in a completely different way from Dympna's. My bargain with Elliott had now been fulfilled. When the dust had settled for all of us, no doubt Dympna would come back to Rosenwell to keep house for Elliott, and I would stay at Highfield, to bring up my little daughter.

It would not be easy at first, but I was determined to get work of some kind, especially during the summer months when the tourist season was at its height. In a few short years, Helen would be old enough to go to school, then her life would be a little like my own when I lived at Highfield with my aunt. She would grow up and be happy, and with God's help, she would not make my mistakes.

'She needs a rest first,' Elliott decided firmly, 'before making that journey, and I want to talk to her. I . . . I should never have doubted her . . . my own sister. I should never have believed . . .'

I could see the hurt in his eyes, and I wanted to comfort him, but I felt I no longer had the right, so I said nothing. Later I knew that in this I was failing Elliott. He needed that comfort. He stared at me for a long time.

'I owe you my thanks . . . I owe you more than I can ever repay.'

'It was all part of the bargain,' I said.

'What?'

'The bargain we made, when I promised to look after Dympna in . . . in return for our marriage. I looked after her to the best of my ability, and now it's all over. I'm glad it has worked out so well for you. You'll be able to marry properly after . . . after our divorce . . . and you can have children. You'll be happy now.'

He was looking at me strangely, and rubbing his forehead with his fingers.

'I don't . . . ' he began, then nodded again. 'We'll talk about it another time. I think you need to rest as well. You look . . . strained. It's all been rather much for you, hasn't it?'

I made no reply. I no longer felt close to Elliott now that I was building a hard protective shell around me against the hurt which was bound to come.

'I must go now,' he said, and bent to

kiss my cheek. 'Whatever the outcome, I can only thank you, though I feel shattered and bewildered myself. For so many years I thought Gerald a . . . a sort of saint or something. He certainly looked like it. I can't get used to the glimpse of the devil I saw in him. And to think that Dympna . . . my own sister . . . had to live with that all these years, and had to watch me support *him* against *her*.'

'Don't blame yourself too much,' I said, quietly. 'It took a woman to see what was behind the façade, and to appreciate the truth.'

'A very perceptive woman. He's had the nursing staff at the hospital, and even Mrs. Sutton eating out of his hand. Stella, too. She thought . . . well, never mind what Stella thought . . . we'll talk later, Berris. Have a good rest, darling.'

The endearment made my heart leap, but it meant nothing. He always called Helen his little darling.

I was deathly tired, too tired to sleep

for a while, then I slid into a nightmare world, grotesque with saint-like faces which crumpled into malevolent grinning images. I thought that Elliott was in my room, smoothing the damp hair on my forehead, but after a while I began to wake up, feeling more refreshed, and to know that a heater had been left on in my bedroom which always meant dreams and fantasies for me.

Mrs. Sutton came in with a tray of tea, and the advice that I had to stay in bed until Gerald Moryson had gone. Dympna, too, was resting on Elliott's instructions, and Ena Makin was looking after my baby.

'What a to-do,' Mrs. Sutton said, pulling the curtains. 'Gracious, but your room's stuffy, Miss Berris. Shall I open a window? It was chilly in the night and Mr. Elliott felt you should have a heater. He's forgot to turn it off.'

'Is he here?' I asked. 'Hasn't he left for the office?'

'After Mr. Moryson goes. They're

waiting for an ambulance now. Right wrathful he is, shouting and screeching against Miss Dympna. Showing his true colours now. That nurse has given notice. He turned on her when she was all smarm over him. It's just like he's been putting a lot of effort into making himself pleasant to us all, and now the lid's off and he's letting all the steam out. It don't smell too sweet either.'

Elliott drove off after the ambulance had gone, and I dressed quickly and hurried to Dympna's room. She, too had slept but only after Elliott had given her the sedative left by the doctor. Now she was stirring, and sitting up, her eyes bewildered.

'Wh . . . what? What's happening?'

'Nothing now. Elliott has removed Gerald. You're really free now, dear. If I were you, I'd get your solicitor on to it right away.'

She sat up in bed, staring at me.

'I used to think I would feel a different person if I were ever free again, but I don't. Not really. I suppose it started to come about gradually after you brought me home from hospital. Better that way.'

'Do you want to go back to Highfield for a week or two? We could both go in the Mini, and take Helen. This time we can really enjoy a holiday. Now your real problems have gone . . . '

I thought of my own problem . . . small compared with Dympna's . . . and of Elliott's. His were the greater. It was one thing to be married if you had a valid excuse for not living as a married person, and quite another now that the valid excuse had gone. I would make it easy for him. I would slip quietly out of his life, and make my home at the cottage. He would be free to build a new life of his own.

During the morning I packed all the things I wanted to keep, mainly Helen's clothes and toys. I had always chosen my own clothes with care so that I had not a great deal to pack, but they were of good quality and would stand hard wear and tear at Highfield.

Dympna had spent some time on the telephone, and I knew she had got in touch with her solicitor, and as she later informed me, had discussed putting her house up for sale. It was in her name, having been bought with her money, with Elliott taking an active interest.

That was probably why Gerald had not ensured that the deeds were in his hands, and not hers, Dympna told me. She had never visualised a time when Gerald would not be living there, and she would be free to sell.

Unlike me she only packed a couple of small cases, and seemed to presume that my luggage was mainly for Helen.

'We'll be back soon,' she said, confidently, 'after things have settled down. I've made an appointment to see Wilson and Gray at the end of the month. I'd better have a look over the house, too, before the final details are settled. I . . . I might even decide to give it to Gerald. It would be worth it to feel free of him, and to free my conscience.'

‘Can’t he pay you something for it? Hasn’t he any money of his own?’

‘Of course he has. His first wife was wealthy and he got the lot. But it was never enough for Gerald. He wouldn’t spend a penny while I was around to provide the bottomless purse.’

‘Then let him sort himself out,’ I told her, and she smiled sadly.

‘It’s so easy when you’re young Berris. Everything is so cut and dried.’

I was learning what it was like to grow older.

The journey north was becoming familiar now that I had driven north a few times. Elliott had telephoned and said he would be staying in town a few days, passing on the message via Mrs. Sutton. He seemed to think we would still be resting.

I wandered round the lovely old house which had been mine for a few short months, while Makin helped to dump our luggage in the car, then I made the break quickly and cleanly, forcing myself to concentrate on driving while Dympna held Helen who was whimpering a little as though sensing my restless mood.

At a Motorway Service Station I phoned ahead to Mrs. Shorrock, who sounded surprised at our quick 'about turn', though she asked no questions, no doubt knowing by now that the answers would lack very much information. She was pleased to hear my sister-in-law was with me again, and I knew that Dympna had made a friend.

We were both too tired to talk very much, however, as the small car ate up the miles, then once again I was driving over my beloved mountains. At least I was coming back to a home I loved.

'We'll soon be there now,' I told Dympna, who moved stiffly beside me, and grunted a reply.

Mrs. Shorrock was waiting for us, taking Helen who was fretful, and I helped Dympna up to bed.

'We'll see to our unpacking in the morning,' I suggested. 'Get into bed and I'll bring you a hot drink.'

'But I should be the one to do all that. You've had enough,' she protested.

I couldn't tell her I was only on my feet through sheer will-power, and I mustn't stop a moment till everything was done. Mrs. Shorrock, bless her, saw that the baby was comfortable, then she ordered me to bed as well, saying she would see to the hot milk for all of us.

I laid my aching head on my pillow and this time the dreams stayed away. This time I slept as though I would never wake again.

* * *

I suppose that deep inside I had hoped that Elliott would not let me go so easily, and I had secret dreams of his coming to Highfield and asking me to return to Rosenwell as his true wife. But after a day or two, I knew that was just wishful thinking. Beyond a curt message to say he was held up in London, we did not hear from him, and I began to gather the shreds of my life around me and to make a routine which, hopefully, would bring me contentment and perhaps even a form of happiness one day.

I knew that the true happiness of being loved by the man I loved would be denied me, but I had learned a lot over the past few months. I was young, and time can heal even the most vicious wounds, though there are scars which always show.

It was all happening to Dympna. Each day she was the one to be up with the lark, helping to clean the house, cook our meals, and take Helen for walks in her small folding pram. Sometimes we took the car into Penrith, Keswick or Carlisle, spending a few hours in the pretty shops, and Dympna even found great joy in packing a picnic, and driving off to view the beautiful scenery of the Lake District.

'It's marvellous,' she said. 'I'm beginning to feel part of it. I can look for ever at Skiddaw and feel that I'm a small part of it . . . though don't ask me to explain.'

I smiled at her enthusiasm, though I was at the lowest ebb of my own reactions, and could not delight in everything around me, as Dympna was doing. She looked younger each day and soon it was easy to see the girl she had been, and to be incensed all over again by Gerald Moryson's treatment of a charming sensitive girl. Why couldn't Elliott have seen, squarely, what was happening, and not be so blinded by an evil man? For the first time I wanted to criticize him, but somehow the knowledge of his faults only made him dearer to me. He was as human as I was myself.

'Cheer up,' Dympna said. 'Elliott will soon be home from London, then you'd better go back to Rosenwell. You've been here long enough. You're missing him too much.'

'I'm no longer missing him at all,' I said, angrily. 'You might as well know now as later . . . I've left Elliott. I'm home to Highfield permanently.'

She stared.

'You're joking! Surely . . . surely now that he knows I'm not pot . . . you know . . . he'll want to start a new life with you. I've been feeling so happy for both of you.'

'Not with me,' I said. 'Get that out of your head. I . . . I suspect he's always really loved Stella Sutton. I don't know if anything will come of that . . . if Paul will release Stella. It won't be hard to have our marriage annulled. It was only a business arrangement anyway.'

'But I thought you loved Elliott.'

'What's that got to do with it?'

I stared at her, feeling the angry tears in my eyes. She looked great. I felt like an old hag. Anyone looking at both of us would choose her as the younger!

'Fight for him,' she urged. 'Go to London. Tell him you want to stay with him, but don't just hand my brother on a plate to that woman. What's the good of finally finding the courage to put my own life straight, if it leaves his in a mess.'

'Well, it *has* left his in a mess. He's stuck with me.'

'He loves you. I know it.'

'Rubbish.'

'And you love him. I've always known that.'

'Oh . . . Dympna! . . . do shut up! Just . . . just don't go on and on. I'll get over it. If one waits long enough the long dreary road takes a turn. Sometimes it's for the worse, but sooner or later there's a bright spot. There will be . . . for Helen and me . . . so don't be too sorry for us. I could be a young girl, struggling on my own with a baby in some sort of bed-sit. Instead I have Highfield.'

'And it's gorgeous,' said Dympna. 'But I only feel I have a right to be here if you're my true sister-in-law.'

'Then you should know by now that you can't have all you want,' I said, shortly.

I was tired, my nerves ragged, or I would never have gone for her. She went very quiet, and that afternoon she slipped out for a walk on the fells, and two hours later I began to get anxious. She was rarely out longer than an hour.

I played with Helen, my eyes on the clock, then on the gradually darkening skies. Helen dropped off to sleep in her pram, and hurriedly I dressed in my warm fell-walking clothing and boots, finding my survival kit just in case, and hurried along, pushing the pram to Mrs. Shorrock's cottage.

'Mrs. Moryson has gone out walking and hasn't come back,' I told her. 'I'm going to find her. If we aren't back in an hour, then maybe you could get in touch with Mountain rescue.'

I love tramping my fells. Within a few miles radius I know every step, every inch of the way. Soon I had covered all paths which were known to me, calling repeatedly for Dympna and ringing a handbell. I watched the sun beginning to sink into the Solway, long fingers of scarlet, pink and silver stretching across the sky.

Normally exertion has no effect on me, but worry was making my heart beat furiously and finally I was almost sobbing her name.

'Dympna!'

I clanged the bell, aware of the dampness of hill fog beginning to close around me. If I didn't know my way so well, recognising land marks, I would be feeling helpless on my own account, but now my fears were all for my sister-in-law.

Suddenly I saw a dark figure looming up and I shouted thankfully. It would be difficult for me to guide us home, but so long as we were together, I could help us both to keep warm until we were found. Though I would not give up till I had lost my own system of well-known landmarks.

'Dympna! Thank God I've found you. Where . . . ?'

'It's me, not Dympna.'

I almost stumbled with shock as Elliott came towards me and took me into his arms.

'Dympna's home. I saw her on the roadway and gave her a lift back to the cottage. My car is over this way on top of that hill road. We'll just make it if we hurry.'

Together we stumbled through the mist and I was beginning to think we has lost the roadway entirely, when the swirling fog cleared a little and I recognised our whereabouts.

'Over there,' I shivered.

In spite of my clothing, the damp was seeping into my bones, and I knew Elliott was equally cold. It tended to make his trouser legs stick, chilling him down.

But now that I had found the road, we made good speed for the car.

'I shall see Dympna about this when we get back,' Elliott said, grimly. 'I thought she had really found herself and learned good sound common sense and competence.'

'She has,' I said, quickly. 'We . . . we just had a small difference of opinion. She went to work it off!'

'What about?'

'You,' I said, reluctantly. 'She . . . she thinks I ought to try to hang on to our marriage. I feel it's time you had something for yourself. It's time to choose what *you* want.'

He settled me into the car, and switched on the engine, and the marvellous warmth began to flow round us.

'I'm glad you feel that way,' said Elliott. 'I choose you.'

'Don't go on being honourable,' I said, feeling tears on my cheeks.

'I'm being selfish,' he said. 'I love you, Berris darling, and if I can't have you, then I'll have nobody. We have a good marriage. Couldn't we make it a perfect one? What do you feel, darling? Am I too old for you? I thought it would not matter now you've grown up, and taken on responsibility so well.'

I bit my lip.

'You're sure it isn't just gratitude for sorting Dympna out?'

He pulled me into his arms and kissed me.

'What do you think?'

'I think you should do that again.'

Elliott roared with laughter.

'That's my girl. Only I want to hear if you love me or not.'

'I love you.'

I could feel him shivering even as he held me, and insisted that we drove home.

'What about Stella Sutton?' I asked.

'Stella?'

'Yes. I thought you loved her, Elliott darling. I was jealous.'

'I did find her attractive,' he admitted, 'but she married Paul when she found out my views on marriage and a family. Now . . . well, now I thank Heaven for being *made* to wait. I always found your funny little face attractive, but I might not have recognised real love if we had not gone through all this together.'

'Have you arranged things for Dympna?'

His voice went grim. 'Certainly. I'll never stop blaming myself, though there's no need to feel sorry for her now. I've never seen her look better.'

But Dympna could look even better, as we found out when we ran into the cottage hand in hand. There was no need to tell her anything, and it was she who made plans for both of us, which seemed to involve, chiefly, a second honeymoon while she kept Helen at Highfield.

'We'll be splendid here for a month or two. Mrs. Shorrock will help, and she's so used to the car now.'

'But you should be getting on with your own life, Dympna,' I protested, 'not baby-sitting for me.'

'Us,' said Elliott, who had picked Helen up, laughing as she grasped one of his ears in her tiny hand. 'Who's Daddy's best girl?'

The baby grinned with delight, then I had to find a tissue to wipe her mouth since she was teething. I felt as free as a bird, as a rush of happiness swept through me, even as the North Wind sometimes swept through our barn cleansing and refreshing.

'Where do you want to go for a much-delayed honeymoon darling?' Elliott asked.

'Highfield,' I chose, 'then Rosenwell.'

'Not good enough. How about Hawaii? Isn't that how it all began?'

I was about to shake my head. I had no very happy memories of Hawaii, and the aftermath of my last trip there. Then I paused. Hadn't it given me Helen . . . then Elliott? . . . and even Dympna whom I had come to love? Every woman needs a woman friend to care for, as well as her man.

'Hawaii would be wonderful,' I said.

And it was.

THE END

Mary Warmington is a pseudonym
of Mary Cummins
who also writes as Jane Carrick

We do hope that you have enjoyed reading this large print book.

Did you know that all of our titles are available for purchase?

We publish a wide range of high quality large print books including:
Romances, Mysteries, Classics
General Fiction
Non Fiction and Westerns

Special interest titles available in large print are:
The Little Oxford Dictionary
Music Book, Song Book
Hymn Book, Service Book

Also available from us courtesy of Oxford University Press:
Young Readers' Dictionary
(large print edition)
Young Readers' Thesaurus
(large print edition)

For further information or a free brochure, please contact us at:

Other titles in the
Linford Romance Library:

CONVALESCENT HEART

Lynne Collins

They called Romily the Snow Queen, but once she had been all fire and passion, kindled into loving by a man's kiss and sure it would last a lifetime. She still believed it would, for her. It had lasted only a few months for the man who had stormed into her heart. After Greg, how could she trust any man again? So was it likely that surgeon Jake Conway could pierce the icy armour that the lovely ward sister had wrapped about her emotions?